Alice Gardner

Synesius of Cyrene

Philosopher and Bishop

Alice Gardner

Synesius of Cyrene
Philosopher and Bishop

ISBN/EAN: 9783337068400

Printed in Europe, USA, Canada, Australia, Japan

Cover: Foto ©Raphael Reischuk / pixelio.de

More available books at **www.hansebooks.com**

The Fathers for English Readers.

SYNESIUS OF CYRENE,

PHILOSOPHER AND BISHOP.

By ALICE GARDNER,

RESIDENT LECTURER, NEWNHAM COLLEGE, CAMBRIDGE.

"Ἅπας γὰρ βίος ἀρετῆς ὕλη.
Synesius, "De Providentia," I., c. xiii.

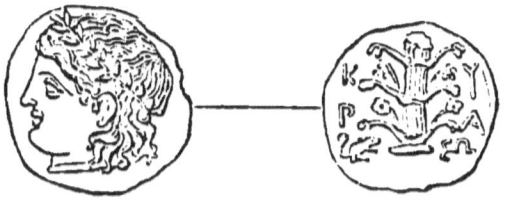

COIN OF CYRENE
Obverse : Head of Apollo.
Reverse : Silphium-plant : jerboa below.

PUBLISHED UNDER THE DIRECTION OF THE TRACT COMMITTEE.

LONDON :
SOCIETY FOR PROMOTING CHRISTIAN KNOWLEDGE,
NORTHUMBERLAND AVENUE, CHARING CROSS, S.W. ;
34, QUEEN VICTORIA STREET, E.C. ;
26, ST. GEORGE'S PLACE, HYDE PARK CORNER, S.W.
BRIGHTON : 135, NORTH STREET.
NEW YORK : E. & J. B. YOUNG & Co.
1886.

TO

PERCY GARDNER, Litt.D.

THIS BOOK IS AFFECTIONATELY DEDICATED,

BY HIS SISTER AND PUPIL,

THE AUTHOR.

PREFACE.

———◇———

This little work is based chiefly on a study of the letters and the other literary productions of Synesius. The references given are to the numbers of chapters and of letters in the Migne edition of 1859, which contains the notes of Dionysius Petavius. Modern readers who wish to study some of the treatises of Synesius should read the elegant translations into German made by Krabinger, which are accompanied by a revised text and copious notes.

The other book that has been principally used is the valuable little treatise in Latin of Theodor Clausen, "De Synesio." This work is full of information and has very numerous references, and the labours of the author to establish a chronological basis for the subject are most helpful to the student. But, though generally sound in his historical criticisms, and kindly disposed towards the object of his treatise, Clausen is wanting in sympathy with the mystic and Hellenic element in the character and the opinions of Synesius.

A far more searching criticism, expressed in more pleasing and popular form, is to be found in Richard Volkmann's "Synesius von Cyrene"—the work of a man deeply versed in the school of philosophy which Synesius represents. If this most valuable and interesting little work were better known in England, our present labour would have been superfluous. But a glance at Volkmann's book will convince the reader that it has in no sense furnished the basis for the sketch which is now submitted to the public.

In the free translation of two hymns given in the Appendix, an attempt has been made to give the

English reader a general notion of the religious poetry
of Synesius, not to present an imitation of his classical
metres.

ALICE GARDNER.

CAMBRIDGE,
October, 1885.

[*Note.*—Although this work does not properly belong to the
Series, "The Fathers for English Readers," it has been
thought advisable, owing to the light which it throws
upon an interesting period of Church History, to include
it in that set.—EDITORIAL SECRETARY, S.P.C.K.]

CONTENTS.

CHAPTER I.   PAGE

BIRTH AND EDUCATION OF SYNESIUS — HIS
POLITICAL AND SOCIAL SURROUNDINGS......... I

CHAPTER II.

SYNESIUS AS PATRIOT — HIS EMBASSY TO CON-
STANTINOPLE 22

CHAPTER III.

SYNESIUS AS COUNTRY GENTLEMAN 49

CHAPTER IV.

SYNESIUS AS PHILOSOPHER........................ 71

CHAPTER V. PAGE

SYNESIUS AS BISHOP-ELECT OF PTOLEMAIS......... 91

———

CHAPTER VI.

SYNESIUS AS WORKING BISHOP 117

———

CHAPTER VII.

SYNESIUS AS CHAMPION OF THE CHURCH 141

———

CHAPTER VIII.

LAST DAYS OF SYNESIUS—CONCLUSION 161

———

APPENDIX.

I. TWO HYMNS BY SYNESIUS 171

II. CHRONOLOGICAL SUMMARY 176

SYNESIUS OF CYRENE.

CHAPTER I.

BIRTH AND EDUCATION OF SYNESIUS—HIS POLITICAL
AND SOCIAL SURROUNDINGS.

Νῦν μὲν οὖν, ἐν τοῖς καθ' ἡμᾶς χρόνοις, Αἴγυπτος
τρέφει τὰς Ὑπατίας δεξαμένη γονάς.[1]

THE usefulness of biography to the student of history
is at the present day clearly recognised, even by those
who most strongly repudiate the theory that "the
history of the world is the biography of great men,"
and who are inclined to regard all particular factors
in history as unimportant in comparison with general
causes. For they see that when we desire to estimate
the relative strength of the various forces—political,
social, or moral,—which at any particular period determined the main current of events, we can often
attain to a more intelligent appreciation of these
forces by tracing their operation in the lives and
thoughts of great individuals who were moulded by
them, and who consciously endeavoured to assist or
to thwart them, than by confining ourselves to the
vaguely-directed actions of the inarticulate multitude.

[1] Synesius, Ep. 135.

There is one point, however, which seems scarcely
to have received sufficient attention from biographers
and historians—that the men most typical of a period
are not, as a rule, to be found among those of the
strongest character and the most original genius.   It
is not that the greatest men are " before their age," as
the phrase goes ; but, rather, that natures of the
greatest vigour and intensity devote themselves to
the realisation of one or two leading ideas, and so
remain unsusceptible to many of the influences around
them.   They may be taken to represent the characteristics of some greater or smaller sections of the
community; but do not often reflect the mind of a
whole society.   Thus, it is not the men of strongest
convictions and greatest power of achievement who
embody for us the spirit of their age, but rather those
of the widest sympathies and the most susceptible
temperaments.   These remarks apply pre-eminently
to an age in which a highly complex state of society
affords scope for many heterogeneous intellectual
forces, and to a man of wide culture, of social disposition, of varied experience.   Such a period was the
earliest part of the fifth century of our era, and such
a man was Synesius of Cyrene.

Synesius was born at Cyrene in or about the year
375 A.D.[1]   As our main task in future chapters will
be to exhibit, by tracing the various phases of the life

---

[1] The date of his birth is calculated from that of his election
to the episcopate, when he was probably just about the canonical
age of thirty, and certainly not much above it.   The materials
for determining that date are pretty clear, and fix it at 409 or
410.   See Clausen, " De Synesio."

of the philosopher and bishop Synesius, some of
the chief characteristics of the time in which he
lived, it would be superfluous to attempt here a
general sketch of the circumstances into which he
was born. It may, however, be desirable to remind
those unfamiliar with the history of that confused
intervening period between classical and mediæval
times of some of the principal changes which were
then taking place in the Roman Empire and in the
Christian Church.

About fifty years before Synesius was born, Constantine the Great had inaugurated certain reforms,
and struck out new lines of policy, the portentous
results of which he can only have in part anticipated.
He had founded a new capital, and so shifted the
centre of gravity of the civilised world, and facilitated
the separation of East and West. He had continued and completed the reorganisation begun by
Diocletian of the government of the empire, which
involved the separation of the military from the civil
authorities, the division of the territory of the empire
into præfectures, dioceses, and provinces, the formation
of a select and influential body of court officials, and
the establishment of a regular hierarchy, in which
certain positions of authority were confined to special
ranks of society. At the same time he had departed
from the policy of simple toleration of all religions,
secured by the Edict of Milan in 313, and had gradually brought about the recognition of Christianity as
the established religion of the State. Thus, he had
issued laws abolishing certain heathen rites, enforcing
the observance of Sunday, and ordering the restoration

and enlarging of churches. He had taken a yet more remarkable step, in personally presiding over the great council which had met at Nicæa (325), and drawn up the first definite scheme of Christian doctrine, and had thus acknowledged that the head of the State was deeply concerned in whatever affected vitally the internal organisation of the Church. The half-century following the death of Constantine was filled with peril and adversities, both in Church and State, which put to a severe test both the new arrangements and the men by whose agency they were to be carried out. Some of those barbarous or semi-barbarous nations which hovered on the frontiers of the empire, ready to avail themselves of any signs of weakness or of internal dissension, found their desired opportunity; while the increasing difficulty of keeping up a sufficient military force to defend so extensive a frontier had certainly not been met by the arrangements of Diocletian and of Constantine. The danger from barbarian inroads became more immediately threatening when, just about the time that Synesius was born, a strong and terrible race, the Huns, hitherto unknown to the western world, migrated from their Asiatic home, and forced into Roman lands tribes that otherwise might have been kept for a time aloof,—notably the Alans, who were defeated, and who had to join the Hunnish hosts and the Goths, who then inhabited the regions about the Don, and some of whom were now allowed to settle within the empire. The continued migrations, due to pressure from without, led of necessity to terrible conflicts, and to a decisive defeat of the Romans at Hadrianople. The emperors who

followed Constantine might favourably compare, for
energy and ability, with an equal number of consecu-
tive rulers taken from almost any list of sovereigns, and
some of them—particularly Julian, Gratian, and Theodosius,—had in them elements of heroic greatness. But
their task was too heavy for them. Julian saved Gaul,
for a time, from the Alemanni and Franks, but fell in
an expedition against the revived power of Persia.
Valentinian was able to defend Britain and Gaul, but
was killed during a campaign on the Danube. His
brother Valens fell fighting against the Goths at
Hadrianople, and his son Gratian was murdered by a
usurper set up by the army. Theodosius, indeed, by
his soldier-like qualities, was able to put down pre-
tenders and to check the ravages of the Goths; but
the policy he adopted, of taking the conquered barbarians into his service, was full of peril for the
future. When he died in 395, and the division of the
empire into East and West, temporarily effected on
several previous occasions, became permanent under
his sons Arcadius and Honorius, it needed no very far-
seeing eye to perceive the coming dangers, with which
two indolent youths, bred in the purple, were scarcely
prepared to cope. Everywhere was disorder; in many
places dissatisfaction at the oppression of the governors. Population and prosperity were declining. Nor
was there in the capital a centralised force sufficient
to compensate for the weakness of distant provinces.
The corrupt influences of an Oriental court become
evident from the days of Diocletian downwards. The
extravagance and immorality of the palace were too
potent for the summary reforms of Julian, the well-

meaning but brutal sternness of Valentinian, or the fitful energy of Theodosius. At the time when the empire required the services of her very best men in the posts where they could act most efficiently, it was too often, though not in all cases, by corrupt machinations and backstairs influence that promotions were made both in the Church and in the State.

This same period had been as full of disorders and dangers in the Church as in the State. It comprises the greater part of the Arian controversy, as well as the brief attempt, under Julian, to revive a purified polytheism in opposition to the new faith. Bitter conflicts and violently-contested ecclesiastical elections had afforded to the populations of great cities an outlet for the restless democratic instinct which no longer found a legitimate field in the exercise of civil liberty. Weak natures had been distracted by controversies, and strong characters embittered by persecution. The force of persecution had generally been employed against the side which ultimately prevailed. The Emperor Valens is said[1] to have mitigated his persecution of the Homoousian or Nicene party, owing to the admonitions of the philosopher Themistius, an intimate friend of Julian, who reminded him that among the Greek pagans there were at least three hundred varieties in religious opinions, and suggested that the majesty of the Godhead is made the more manifest by the difficulty which men find in attaining to certain knowledge thereof. But it was the conqueror of the Goths who

---

[1] Socrates, "Ecclesiastical History," iv., 32.

did as much, perhaps, as one man could do to heal
the schism in the Church. Theodosius himself was
baptised in 380 by a bishop of the Nicene faith, and
shortly afterwards he called a council which reaffirmed
that faith and forced all bishops of other persuasions
to resign their sees. There was not henceforth,
however, much active persecution, the Arians being
still allowed to hold their assemblies outside the
walls of towns. But the Arian party was already
much weakened by internal dissensions, and perhaps
its most earnest adherents were to be found amongst
the barbarian Goths, lately converted by the mis-
sionary efforts of Bishop Ulphilas. There were also
Arian factions in some of the great towns of the
East. But their authority was waning, so that within
ten years after the close of the heroic life of
Athanasius—a life full of earnest efforts and temporary failures—the cause which he had valiantly
maintained was recognised as triumphant. But the
evil results of the controversy were everywhere
apparent, both in the polemic fever which burned
throughout ecclesiastical life and favoured the growth
of vagaries of doctrine far more estranged from
Christianity than anything broached by Arius himself,
and in the dangerously-powerful influence of the
court, against which some of the noblest ecclesiastical
characters of this period—notably Ambrose of Milan
and John Chrysostom of Constantinople—had to
contend. In general, this period may be charac-
terised, both in Church and State, as one of overstrain.
In both spheres difficulties were multiplying without
and corruption within. And as the Persians and the

Goths, or even the Huns, were less formidable foes to the empire than the unscrupulousness and rapacity of her own officials, so in the Church no attacks from pagans or heretics could work greater evil than the violent temper and irregular habits engendered in the clergy by the prevalent disorder. It was against these most serious evils, in political and ecclesiastical affairs, that Synesius was called to contend.

Yet, after all, the evils that afflicted the Imperial Government and the Catholic Church did not much affect the life of Synesius in his boyhood and early youth. The society in which he moved was pagan,— or, as it called itself, Hellenic,—and cared nothing for ecclesiastical controversies. And Cyrene was out of the way of the Huns and the Goths. It had, however, many troubles peculiar to its own district. Situated in a region of remarkable beauty, fertility, and commercial accessibility, on the edge of a high table-land, between which and the sea there extended a rich valley, where other prosperous Greek cities had been founded in early times, Cyrene could once have claimed a high position among the cities of the Mediterranean. Herodotus gives an interesting account of the foundation of the colony by Dorians from Thera, afterwards reinforced by other settlers from the Peloponnesus. The agricultural and commercial advance of Cyrene was rapid, and was accompanied by a remarkable intellectual progress. In the time of Herodotus, the art of medicine was cultivated there with greater success than in almost any other place in the known world. Poetry and the arts (especially such as minister to comfort and luxury) were not neglected, and in the early part of the fourth century B.C., Cyrene was the head-quarters of a school of philosophy, founded by Aristippus, a pupil of Socrates, who professed the principle— agreeable to a climate like that of Cyrene—that pleasure is the chief aim of life, together with another, —not easy to reconcile with the former in practice— that men should use pleasures without being mastered by them. But the prosperity of the city was not very long-lived. The rivalry of Carthage was, for a time, decidedly formidable, and from early times its relations with Egypt were often strained. Like most level and fertile districts, Cyrenaica had never opposed a very stout resistance to invaders, so that, after the conquest of Alexander, his general, Ptolemy, was able to annex it to the kingdom of Egypt. The whole region, which, from the five towns which made it important (viz., Cyrene, its port Apollonia, Ptolemais [the port of Barca], Arsinoë, and Berenice), is usually called the Libyan Pentapolis, continued under the rule of the Ptolemies, either as an integral part of the kingdom, or as an appanage under some member of the royal house, till the year 95 B.C., when it fell under the power of Rome, though it was not till 78 B.C. that, in conjunction with Crete, it was formed into a Roman province. Under Constantine, or perhaps under Diocletian, it was separated from Crete and placed under a *præses* (ἡγεμών), who seems[1] to have been under the authority of the *Præfectus Augustalis* of Egypt, who, in his turn,

[1] See evidence in Clausen, "De Synesio," especially reference to Ep. 127.

was subordinate to the Prætorian Præfect of the East.

Of civil liberty in the time of Synesius we find no trace,[1] though the traditions of Cyrene were republican. The old line of kings (the Battiadæ) had been forced to give up all practical authority at the foundation of the constitution of Demonax, who had divided the people into classes according to their origin. All vestiges of these classes as a political institution had long since been swept away—historians generally seem inclined to think they had a very brief existence; but they may have been maintained as a ground of social distinction. Certainly the upper classes were careful to maintain their pedigrees. Synesius himself was very proud of his descent from the royal stock of Sparta, and his delight in being able to trace his ancestry up to Hercules is all the more conspicuous when introduced apologetically,[2] as a pardonable weakness. His whole political tone, as we shall see hereafter, is that of a conscientious aristocrat, who believes both in the privileges and in the responsibilities entailed by high birth. But, apart from historical associations and pleasantness of aspect and climate, Cyrene was not a very desirable place of abode during the early years of Synesius. All the most devastating forces of nature and of man seemed to have been leagued

---

[1] There was a βουλή, but it could not do much, except make complaints.

[2] Ep. 57. See also the account of a blue-blooded old gentleman in Ep. 3.

against the once-favoured city.[1] Inroads of locusts
had frequently destroyed the crops; earthquakes and
plagues had desolated the territory. In the time of
Trajan and Hadrian, there had been a serious insurrection of the Jews (it will be remembered that in the
New Testament we have frequent mention of the
Jews from Cyrene, or from "the parts of Libya about
Cyrene "), which had been put down with such
cruelty as to cause a considerable depopulation. Add
to these troubles the perpetual inroads of barbarous
Libyan tribes, and, worst of all, as most paralysing
to hope and energy, the grinding exactions and
tyranny of the Roman officials, and we cannot wonder
that both a material and an intellectual decline had
set in. These circumstances formed, however, the
determinant factors of the life of Synesius. Had he
been able to obtain a good education at home, he
might not have gone to Alexandria, and so might
never have known Hypatia. Had his country been
prosperous, he would not have been sent on that
embassy which was his first introduction to public
life. And but for the disorders of the times, it is by
no means probable that he would ever have been
raised to the bishopric of Ptolemais.

Of the parents of Synesius, except that they were
persons of wealth and standing, we know nothing.
They probably died while he was a child. He had,
however, a brother and a sister, to whom he was
tenderly attached. His sister, Stratonice, whose
beauty he celebrated in a graceful epigram, became

---

[1] "De Regno," Catastasis i. and ii. Letters, *passim.*

the wife of Theodosius, an official at the Byzantine
Court.[1]   His brother, Euoptius, apparently younger
than himself,[2] was all through his life his dearest and
closest friend ; and as for a considerable portion of
their lives the brothers were separated (Synesius
living at Cyrene, on his country estate, or at Ptolemais, and Euoptius at Alexandria or at the Cyrenaic
port of Phycus), the letters of Synesius to his brother[3]
form the best material that we have for ascertaining
the events of his outward life, and also for acquaint-
ing ourselves with his inward character.[4]   It was
probably in the company of his brother and sister,
and some other playmates and fellow-students,[5] that
he spent his boyhood at Cyrene.   We do not hear of
any masters to whom he owed anything ; and, as he
was not a man likely to forget obligation of any kind,
it seems probable that he was not carefully taught,
but allowed to range freely in a good Greek library.
He certainly loved books all his life, and was widely
read in poetry, history, and philosophy ; yet his

[1] Ep. 75.

[2] The question of the relative ages of the two brothers ought
to be conclusively settled by Ep. 94; but the critical passage is
so worded as to enable scholars to form diametrically opposite
opinions on it.   *Cf.* Volkmann, Clausen, and Druon.

[3] Synesius also calls a certain Anastasius his brother, but does
not mention him in Hymn viii., in which he is praying for all his
nearest relations.

[4] Euoptius seems not to have been entirely worthy of his
brother's affection, *i.e.*, if it was he who succeeded him in the
bishopric of Ptolemais.   The only thing we have recorded of
him is an unreasonable and snarling speech demanding severity
on heretics.   See Neander's " Church History."

[5] Ep. 60.

memory, though quick and ready, was never accurate, and his quotations, even from his beloved Homer, are not always verbally correct. Verbal accuracy, indeed, seemed to him a trifling merit, always to be sacrificed to originality of mind. He even went so far as to regard the corruption of an author's text[1] as a positive advantage, because it stimulates the ingenuity of the reader to amend errors and supply gaps. Could he have foreseen the havoc that succeeding centuries would make in his manuscripts, he might have hesitated to apply his principle to his own case.

But Cyrene, in its material and spiritual decline, could not afford a good mental training to Synesius and Euoptius. They were therefore sent, or perhaps went of their own accord, to study at the great city within a short sea voyage of their home, which was better able than any other at that time—we may almost say than any other city of any time—to supply food and stimulus to eager and growing minds.

It is, perhaps, scarcely possible to overrate the importance of the part which the city of Alexandria has played in the history of civilisation. Her situation admirably fitted her for the function of mediator between East and West, and she was called into being just at the moment when such a mediator was required. But the prescient eye of her founder, though he might safely anticipate her commercial greatness, and might suspect the possibility of her future political importance, could hardly have foreseen that ideas and systems of Greeks and Orientals

---

[1] "Dion," c. xiv., xv.

would there meet for exchange as freely as material products, or that the colony of Jews he admitted into the city would do even more to elevate and broaden Greek thought than to maintain Greek commerce. The sagacious state policy and the intellectual tastes of the kings of the House of Ptolemy raised her to be the commercial and spiritual capital of the world. Under their fostering care were formed the magnificent library, in which, as is well known, the sacred books of the Jews found a place, and the Museum, a kind of university in which many subjects were studied, but in which mathematics and medicine rose to the highest point of excellence. The Museum, though still in existence, had fallen into decline before Synesius came to Alexandria; but the great philosophical school, which had grown up almost independently of it, the last great product of the Greek mind, was still vigorous, and—partly, no doubt, by the remarkable character of its leader,— influential, and even fashionable.

Our task would indeed assume formidable proportions if we were to attempt even a very general sketch of the development of the chief characteristics and tenets of the Neo-Platonic school of Alexandria; [1] and, so far as they were represented by Synesius himself, they will occupy us in a future chapter. A few remarks must here suffice to show the aspect under which philosophy was presented to the mind of Synesius when he first applied himself to the study of the subject. The Alexandrian school has been

[1] For a most interesting history, analysis, and criticism of this school, see Vacherot's " École d'Alexandrie."

called eclectic, and certainly it comprised elements
supplied from very various quarters. But it did not
owe its existence to a shallow taste for adopting the
pleasant and avoiding the disagreeable in all schemes
of thought, without taking the trouble to weed truth
from error and to reject incongruities, so as to form
a system. It sprang rather from a conviction of
the essential unity of the truth, to which earnest
seekers have in all ages been led by different ways ;
of the divine origin and supreme worth of wisdom,
and especially the faculty of contemplation ; and
it aspired to rise, by a life of noble action and
quiet thinking, above the vexations and uncertainties
of the material world, to the blissful fruition of
eternal realities. But, while ready to accept suggestions of truth from all quarters,—to reverence the
mystic lore and practical wisdom of Pythagoras, to
receive all that Aristotle had contributed in examining
the relation of cause and effect and in exalting the
character of pure thought, and to assimilate the
noble moral ideas proclaimed by the Stoics—yet the
strongest inspiration, the widest scope for the minds
of the Alexandrians, was found in the lofty speculations and the "glorious insufficiencies" of Plato.
There were strong affinities between the philosophy
of Plato and that of Philo, the Alexandrian Jew, in
whose writings we find a half-developed doctrine of the
Trinity, and a first attempt to interpret the Hebrew
Scriptures so as to adapt them to the progressive
ideas of a cultivated, critical, and broadly-human
society. Philo was not without influence on some,
at least, of the earliest teachers of the Neo-Platonic

school ;[1] though, in time, a reaction against Orient-
alism set in, and a determination not to let the great
Western thinker be deprived of his due honour.
Meantime, Christianity had been brought to Alexandria, and, under the joint influence of Philo, of Plato,
and of the earliest teachers of Christianity, a school
of Christian thinkers arose, the most eminent of
whom were Clement and Origen, who upheld the
worthiness of philosophy as preparing the way for
faith, and who held very broad and liberal views as
to the interpretation of Scripture and the final salva-
tion of all men.   Some adherents of the Christian
school, notably Origen, attended the lectures of the
real founder of the Neo-Platonic school, Ammonius
Saccas, who lived during the latter part of the second
and the first half of the third century of our era.
This school, the doctrines of which had been fully
developed by Plotinus, was, at the time that Synesius
joined it, presided over by a woman, to whose high
character and brilliant attainments we have con-
verging testimony from divers quarters, the philosopher Hypatia.[2]

The name of Hypatia must at once recall to the
minds of all readers the delightful work [3] in which,
under the form of a romance, a vivid representation

---

[1] Especially Numenius.   See Vacherot's " École d'Alexandrie."

[2] For a clear and interesting statement of all that the sources
tell us about Hypatia, see an article by Roche in " Philologus,"
vol. xv. ; see also Kingsley, " Alexandria and her Schools."

[3] C. Kingsley's " Hypatia ; or, New Foes with an Old
Face."

is given us of this remarkable woman and of her relations to the world around her,—a work by which the name of Synesius himself is probably familiar to many who else would never have heard it. The attractiveness of her character and the pathos of her life are not diminished by being withdrawn from the realm of fiction to that of sober history. If those who insist on strict chronological accuracy, may feel a slight disappointment in learning that, at the time of her death, she must have been considerably advanced in age,[1] and could hardly have attracted the young monk from the Thebaid by the charms of her youthful beauty, they may console themselves with the discovery that a relation, almost precisely like that feigned between Hypatia and Philammon, did actually exist earlier between the same lady and her young pupil from Cyrene. And a most charming pupil Synesius must have been. All his writings during his early life show a bright and quick intellect, a keen sense of humour, a high ideal of life and duty, a hopeful and courageous spirit, and a deeply reverent and religious tone of mind. His gratitude to his teacher and his appreciation of her merits, are shown by the frequency with which, in his letters, he bursts forth in her praises, by the friendly messages he is constantly sending to her and to her family, and by seven letters to her, still extant, expressive of a friendship which no differences in creed or fortune could

---

[1] Synesius was a pupil of Hypatia before 400 A.D. (the year of his embassy), and corresponded with her till after the death of all his children ; and the name of *Mother*, by which he calls her, seems to indicate that she was considerably the elder.

ever cool. There is no trace of anything like gallantry
in these letters of Synesius to Hypatia. We know
from various sources that she was a woman who
always maintained her dignity in her relations with
men, and the reverence with which he regarded her,
placed her for him far above the level of ordinary
women. The letters are not unlike any that a man
of the warm temperament of Synesius might have
written to a man from whom he had learned much,
and whom he honoured much. She had taught him
mathematics,[1] and he writes to ask her to procure
for him some hydrostatic instrument, apparently for
measuring specific gravities. He writes notes of introduction for his friends to her, knowing that she is always
ready to perform kindly services. He grumbles to
her, as he does to his other friends, whenever he is
left for a time without letters. He wishes to go and
see her, as he perpetually desires to see his friends,
but is withheld by public duties. The thought of
her friendship consoles him in his deepest troubles.
He calls her "the illustrious and god-beloved philosopher," addresses her as his "mother, sister, teacher,
constant benefactress." He tells her of his vexations
from carping critics, shows his books to her before
he publishes them, and is always ready to defer to
her judgment.[2] Only on one occasion—and that

---

[1] Her father, Theon, was a mathematician, and a member
of the Museum. All the writings of Hypatia, the names of
which have come down to us, are on mathematical subjects.

[2] Her appreciation of his character, and her sprightly wit,
are shown in her playful name for him — τὸ ἀλλότριον
ἀγαθόν. Ep. 80.

the most critical of his life—we have no record that
he asked or obtained her advice.

As we know that Synesius in his early youth was
a pagan, and that he gradually advanced through
Platonism to Christianity, we should like to know
how far he was at this time acquainted with the
Christian doctrines, or had mixed in the society of
Christian people. The probability seems to be that
during this part of his life there was no distinctly
Christian element among the influences that were
moulding his life and mind. Respecting the attitude
of Hypatia towards Christians, we have not sufficient
material for forming an opinion. It is hardly correct
to regard her as a martyr for polytheism, for the
cause which led to her tragic fate was not her creed,
but the suspicion of the Alexandrian mob that her
influence over the praefect Orestes (a professing
Christian)[1] was preventing him from being reconciled
to the Archbishop Cyril. The relations between
Christians and Pagans (or Hellenes) at Alexandria
afford some puzzling contrasts. On the one hand,
we have the friendly spirit shown by liberal Christians,
like Origen, towards heathen philosophy, and the
tolerant views of philosophers like Libanius, and like
Themistius who compared the different religions of
his time to the various paths in the racecourse by
which the several runners approach the same goal
and the same judge. On the other hand, we have the
proselytising (though not persecuting) efforts of Julian
and the violent and irregular conduct of Alexandrian

See Socrates, " Eccles. Hist.," vii., 15.

bishops and Alexandrian mobs. The fact would seem to be that with the exception of a few ardent natures (for Julian was not supported by any considerable following), Christians and Pagans of the cultivated classes were able to live harmoniously together, except on those occasions when some commotion among a singularly irascible populace, or a headstrong bishop, supported by fanatical monks, called forth the latent seeds of discord. Such an occasion arose in the year 389, and reflects such discredit on a man for whom Synesius afterwards expressed esteem and admiration, that I am inclined to think that he cannot have been in Alexandria at the time, and therefore, if the date given above for his birth be correct, that he must have been at least over fourteen years old before he came to Alexandria. The emperor Theodosius had ordered the Pagan worship to be put down, and the task was carried out by the patriarch Theophilus (a man, as we shall afterwards see, of insincere character as well as violent temper), with a brutality which led to resistance on the part of the Pagans, and an affray in which many were killed or wounded on both sides.[1] Theophilus left only one statue of the god Sarapis, "lest at a future time the heathens should deny that they had ever worshipped such gods." This speech shows either wilful blindness or gross stupidity on the part of Theophilus. He might have known, being acquainted with educated Alexandrian society, that cultivated people no more worshipped the statue of

---

[1] Socrates, " Eccles. Hist.," v., 16.

Sarapis than he himself worshipped the table at which he ministered, or the East to which he turned in prayer. It is difficult to imagine how Synesius can ever have felt respect for such a man, and some of his biographers are inclined to set down all his expressions of regard for him as empty compliment. But it is not impossible that, amid the rapid changes of the times, this unhappy event may have been partially forgotten by the fickle Alexandrians before he came among them.

But, in any case, we have no evidence that Synesius was at this date acquainted with Theophilus, or with any other member of the Alexandrian Church, nor does he seem to have had any acquaintance with the Christian Scriptures. He afterwards acknowledged his deficiency in this respect, and certainly, after he had decisively embraced Christianity, his views on the subject seem to have come mainly from other than biblical sources. But we shall return to this point again. We must turn now to another phase in the life of Synesius, and see him engaged in behalf of his oppressed countrymen, and setting out for the distant Byzantine Court, with the bold design of convincing an indolent autocrat of his obligations to the people over whom he ruled.

C

CHAPTER II.

SYNESIUS AS PATRIOT—HIS EMBASSY TO CONSTANTINOPLE.

Ἔξεστιν οὖν . . . . . μᾶλλον δὲ πᾶσα ἀνάγκη, τὸν αὐτὸν εἶναι καὶ φιλόσοφον καὶ φιλόπολιν, καὶ μηδ' ἀπογινώσκειν τῆς τύχης, ἀλλὰ καὶ προσδοκᾶν τὰ ἀμείνω.[1]

ALL students of history are familiar with the fact that the feeling of patriotism, though always present among the nobler members of a society that is not hopelessly corrupt, assumes widely different forms in different ages and places. Among civilised nations of ancient times, it is chiefly attached to civic liberty and independence. In the most brilliant days of Greece, when the independent states were not, as with us, large tracts of territory, but small, isolated communities,—when political and municipal life were identical,—the attachment felt by the free citizen to his own city was often so strong as to hinder the growth of a wider sentiment of nationality. Community of race, and similarity of institutions, strengthened by a common historical experience, were, nevertheless, often able to create strong bonds of association, especially when common dangers threatened from without. Apart from traditional

[1] Synesius, Ep. 103.

sentiment, and from mere attachment to locality—
the tendency in human nature always to regard the
near as more interesting than the distant—the most
constant elements in the patriotic feeling seem to be
the desires for political liberty and for national independence. But in the time of the Roman Empire,
these two elements must have been almost entirely
wanting. The patriotism of men like Synesius was
chiefly based on historical associations, and was
directed, not to civil or national aggrandisement, but
to the mitigation of the evils from which their
countries were suffering. In Synesius himself the
object of patriotic devotion was complex. While his
native city, Cyrene, the burial-place of his ancestors,
was, in her down-trodden estate, always beloved and
lamented by him above any other city, he felt a keen
interest in the fortunes of those neighbouring Greek
cities which, though formerly independent of Cyrene,
had undergone similar vicissitudes, and were now
placed under the same provincial administration.
Even Alexandria, from his occasional periods of
residence there, seems to have acquired a claim on
his affections, so that, as he said, he regarded all
Alexandrians as, in a sense, his fellow-citizens. But,
above all, Synesius felt himself to be a Greek of
Dorian blood. At a much later period of his life,
he prayed[1] that his deeds might be worthy of the
old glories of Cyrene, and of Sparta. And under
the Roman Empire, all Hellenic feeling tended to a
loyal support of the imperial authority,—the great

---

[1] Hymn v.

2 C

bulwark of the civilised world against Barbarian
inroads. So that all the political aspirations of
Synesius were directed to wants, order, and good
government for his own city and province, and
security from invasion for the countries under Roman
rule.

But the interest which he felt in public affairs did
not inspire Synesius with a wish to enter the employment of the State, or to undertake the duties of those
inferior posts by which men could rise to the highest
dignities of the empire. The open way to the public
service was through the law-courts, and Synesius was
occupying himself with more congenial studies than
that of the law, and either felt or affected a Platonic
contempt for public speaking, while he would utterly
have scorned the ignoble means by which, at that
time, many public men rose to power. But even if
he had desired to rise to the governorship of his
native province, such an honour would have been
impossible for him. It was the policy of the Empire
to allow as few personal ties as possible between the
civil governors and the provinces over which they
ruled. No native of any province could be appointed
governor over it, nor might any governor acquire
landed property, or contract a marriage within his
sphere of jurisdiction. And so much more probable
appeared the abuse than the legitimate use by the
ruler of intimate personal relations with his subjects,
that this law was strongly upheld by Synesius in the
interests of the Pentapolitans themselves.[1]   It was

* Ep. 73.

otherwise with the function undertaken by Synesius, one implying no special training nor any qualifications but a certain amount of wealth and leisure, and the respect and confidence of his fellow-citizens. He was appointed an ambassador, or delegate, charged to bring before the ears of the emperor Arcadius the grievances of the city of Cyrene.

Almost the only political privilege left to the cities and provincial districts under the Roman Empire was that of making formal remonstrances. This privilege was probably regarded as a useful safety-valve for disaffection, and the whole system of electing delegates and presenting petitions had been carefully protected and minutely elaborated.[1] We have no information as to the circumstances which induced the Senate of Cyrene to choose Synesius as its spokes-man. He must have returned from Alexandria some time before 397 A.D., the date which may be asserted with tolerable certainty[2] as that of his starting for Constantinople, and have made himself well-known and generally respected in his native city. It has been conjectured[3] that he was summoned home by the death of his father. This, however, is entirely uncertain, as we have no private letters or other writings of Synesius which we can with certainty assign to a date before his embassy. Nor can we

---

[1] See Theodosian Code, book xii., t. xii.

[2] He spent three years in Thrace, and Aurelian was consul when he returned. (See Hymn iii.; "De Insomniis," c. ix.; Ep. 61, &c.) Many other arguments point to the same con-clusion.

[3] Volkmann, "Synesius von Cyrene," ch. i.

even be certain what were the exact instructions with
which he was furnished, or the particular demands
he was desired to make. In his speech before the
emperor, to which we shall have to direct our attention, the grievances brought forward are stated broadly
and generally, in such a manner as to prepare the
way for more definite requests. But, besides that
speech, the letters and other writings of Synesius,
together with what we know from other sources of
the state of the Cyrenaica at that time, enable us to
conjecture that what he had to demand was some
remission of taxes, more severity towards those who
obstructed the course of justice, possibly a commission
to inquire into such obstructions, and some increase
in the force for military defence.

It seems probable that the Pentapolis would have
been better governed, if it had been more independent
of Egypt in civil, more dependent in military affairs.
The Praefectus Augustalis was not necessarily a man
of high character and standing, so that the dignity of
the governor of the Pentapolis, who, as already stated,
was amenable to his authority, was of a very inferior
kind. This latter functionary was able to use great oppression, especially in matters of taxation, for though
the amount required for imperial expenses was pre-
scribed by the court, the mode of assessment must
have been in part determined locally, and a very large
portion must have found its way into the pockets of intermediary officers, on whom the bonds of traditional
rule did not lie very heavily.[1] Even in time of peace,
rich men could set the laws at defiance. A very con-

----

[1] Ep. 38.

siderable number of the extant letters of Synesius are recommendations of persons who have suffered wrong, or requests of protection for such as are likely to fall into evil hands. Two of these letters[1] are addressed to the Praefectus Augustalis himself, but that dignitary does not seem to have had sufficient authority over the Pentapolis to secure justice, except in individual cases.

But the military defence of that region would have been, Synesius thought,[2] more effective, if it were under the same authority as that of Alexandria. The want of proper military organisation and of responsible military authorities will be seen when we come to the martial episodes in the life of Synesius.

Two other points respecting the embassy of Synesius are open to doubt. We do not know whether he was accompanied by colleagues, as was usually the case with delegates, for none are mentioned in his letters or his speech. Nor can we say whether the cause he had to maintain, was that of Cyrene only, or that of the whole Pentapolis. He says that he was sent by the Senate of Cyrene, but he elsewhere speaks of cities (in the plural) as being benefited by his mission. The probability[3] is that, while he was specially commissioned by Cyrene, he was accompanied by delegates from the other four towns, and that these did not remain with him during the whole dreary three years, for he certainly returned without them.[4]

The authority with which he was clad raised the social standing of every ambassador. In journeying to the capital, he was allowed the use of a public con-

---

' Ep. 29, 30.   ³ See Clausen, " De Syn.," lib. i.

² Ep. 94.   ⁴ Ep. 61.

veyance, and after his return home, he enjoyed certain
immunities besides honorary distinctions. More important for Synesius than any such advantages, were
the valuable friendships he made or renewed with
some of the leading men in Byzantine society. Chief
among these were the praetorian praefect Aurelian,
Anthemius, who afterwards ruled the empire during
the minority of Theodosius II., Troilus, the philosopher, and a certain Pylaemenes, of whose learning
Synesius had so high an opinion that he generally
became stilted and affected in style in the otherwise
pleasing and interesting letters which he addressed
to him. Considering the social advantages and the
fair measure of success which ultimately attended
his mission; considering, also, that Synesius was
not entirely free from vanity, and always took a pardonable pleasure in contemplating the results of his
own actions, we might expect that in after days he
would look back upon his first public function with a
feeling of pride and delight such as Cicero felt in his
consulship. Far from this, however, he subsequently
regarded these years as a dreary and miserable time
from which he was thankful to have escaped. This
fact is due to the series of painful and perilous events
which occurred while Synesius was in Constantinople,
and which hampered his task and gave him an un-
pleasant insight into the most desperate condition of
the Eastern Empire.

The Emperor Arcadius was a most unworthy son
of the great Theodosius. Without any strength of
character, entirely led by a domineering minister, or
by his clever, but unreasonable wife Eudoxia, he was

capable—as is often the case with weak natures—of occasional acts of great unfairness and cruelty. The great minister who ruled emperor and empire at the beginning of the reign—Rufinus the Gaul, very soon fell through the enmity of the far abler minister of the Western Empire, Stilicho the Vandal.[1] From that time, far the most powerful man in the East was the eunuch Eutropius, who, besides other offices, held the consulate of the year 399 A.D., and who notoriously sold all the dignities and privileges of the State to the highest bidder. The fall of this man came about in a very tragic manner. In 399 A.D., the dangers attendant on the policy of Theodosius in allowing the Goths to settle within the limits of the empire, showed themselves in an alarming manner. Tribigild, the leader of a colony of Goths established in Phrygia, became discontented with the treatment he was receiving from the emperor, and began to sack the cities and devastate all the surrounding country with his barbarous hosts. He defeated the imperial general sent against him, and threatened the neighbourhood of the capital itself. This region had been intrusted for protection to another Goth, the chief commander Gainas, who, whether or no originally concerned in the insurrection of Tribigild, magnified the power of the barbarian chief, and persuaded the emperor to attend to his demands. One of the first of these was the life of Eutropius. This powerful minister had made himself hateful, by his deeds of tyranny and oppression, to all respect-

---

[1] The fact of his Vandal extraction is not beyond dispute, resting mainly on the testimony of Orosius.

able citizens. In the relentless pursuit of his victims he had disregarded the privileges of sanctuary allowed to the churches since the days of Constantine, and so had raised up a formidable enemy in the bishop of Constantinople, John Chrysostom. This notable man was, at the time of the embassy of Synesius, one of the most influential persons in Constantinople. He had reluctantly been brought from Antioch to fill this important see. In early life he had been a pupil of Julian's friend Libanius, and had begun to study the law with a view to preparing himself for a public career. Had he pursued his original course, he would probably have distinguished himself first as a brilliant orator, and later as an incorruptible magistrate. But the desire for spiritual perfection drove him into a life of loneliness and asceticism, and when he returned to human society, it was to the church that he devoted those talents which found there a wider scope than they could ever have obtained in the State. Stern and inflexible towards the immoral and unruly—especially among the clergy—perfectly fearless in his denunciations of folly in high places, yet singularly forbearing towards the erring, and a constant champion of the weak, the golden-tongued bishop was a power in the city that Eutropius might well have feared to disregard. But the opposition of a man like Chrysostom was probably far less formidable to Eutropius than a grudge harboured against him by the empress Eudoxia, who persuaded her husband to accede to the request of Tribigild. The wretched man was forced to fly, and he took refuge in the very place whence he had caused his own enemies to be hunted, and cowered beneath the altar of the principal church of Constantinople.

Never perhaps in any place of worship was there a more impressive scene than in that church of St. Sophia at the public assembly held next after the flight of Eutropius. It must have seemed to the witnesses as if all that was vilest in the dying empire, all that was noblest in the rising church, stood confronted in the persons of these two men. Having ascended the pulpit, Chrysostom began by pointing out to the fallen minister, in words that to some[1] appeared unduly harsh, the desperate state to which he had brought himself by the neglect of timely advice. And now the mob of the circus, which he had pampered and trusted, was clamouring for his blood; the church which he had persecuted alone protected him. Then turning to the congregation, he made a powerful appeal on behalf of the miserable man before them. They might fancy that the presence of such a wretch polluted the church itself. But were the feet of Christ polluted by the sinful woman fleeing from her accusers, or did not his presence sanctify the criminal herself? And how could these Christian people pray to be forgiven as they forgave their debtors, or approach to take the body of Him who said "Father, forgive them, for they know not what they do," unless they could forgive this suppliant who had fled to the church for refuge. Let them all join in beseeching God and

---

[1] *E.g.*, to Socrates.

the emperor that safety might be accorded to him,
that he might yet have an opportunity of amending
his wretched life. The eloquent appeal was partially
successful. Eutropius was not killed then and there,
but induced to come out and to go into exile in
Cyprus, whence he was not long afterwards recalled
to be put to death.

But the fall of Eutropius only marked the end of
the first act of the tragedy. The news soon came that
Gainas himself had united his forces with those of Tribigild, and that the two leaders were marching on the
capital. The emperor consented to meet the rebellious
general in the church of St. Euphemia, at Chalcedon,
just opposite to Constantinople. Gainas demanded
that his Goths should be admitted into the capital,
and that two of the chief persons in the imperial service,
Aurelian and Saturninus, should be given up to his
mercy. The baseness of the emperor, and the willing
patriotism of the consulars, led them to accede to the
request. John Chrysostom now used his persuasive
powers on behalf of nobler fugitives than Eutropius.
Aurelian and Saturninus had their lives spared, but
were sent into banishment, and seem to have remained in exile for some months. Meanwhile, the
Goths were admitted into Constantinople. Tempted
by the hope of plunder, they attempted to set fire to
the imperial palace, but their design was betrayed. At
length, Gainas himself left the city, and attempted to
gather his forces outside. But a sudden panic seems
to have seized them. The citizens shut their gates.
Many barbarians took refuge in their church,
which, contrary to the laws of the empire, had been

appropriated, though within the city precincts, to
the Arian worship. Multitudes were killed. Gainas
himself was able to withdraw ; but many of his ships
were destroyed in the Hellespont. Another Goth,
Fravitta, loyal to the imperial cause, undertook the
defence of the provinces nearest home. Gainas carried on war against some of the Thracian cities, but
perished at the hands of the Huns. Thus, a most
formidable danger to the empire had been averted,
not so much by any remarkable courage or prudence
on the part of the government, as by the want of
clearness and unity of purpose among the insurgents,
and by a happy combination of accidents. The failure
of the Goths became a favourite subject for the literary
circles of Constantinople. Court poets probably used
it to magnify the scarcely deserved reputation of the
emperor. To Synesius it suggested deeper thoughts
as to the rottenness of a state not founded on right-
eousness, and the limits of providential intervention
on behalf of men.

It is not wonderful, that under these cirumstances,
Synesius could not obtain a speedy and satisfactory
hearing. Lying before the entrance to the government
offices, on a thick Oriental rug,—the beautiful or useful
qualities of which so charmed one of the government
clerks, that he begged Synesius to leave it to him
on his departure,—he waited long for an audience.
He had first to make out his case to the practorian
praefect. It was probably not till Aurelian obtained
this office, at the beginning of the year 399 A.D.,
that he was admitted to the imperial presence. The
exact time at which his oration was delivered is

doubtful. Internal evidence would suggest a date between the first threats of a Gothic rising and the final catastrophe. The occasion of the delivery was the presentation of a crown of gold, or of gold weighing sufficient to form a circlet, the customary gift of delegates from the provinces. But the young philosopher was determined not to confine himself to mere compliment, now that he had an opportunity of expressing, in the highest quarters, his ideas as to the evils of the time and their remedies. He seems to have been lately enriching his mind with suggestions and illustrations from his favourite author, the rhetor Dio Chrysostom, who composed at least four orations on the subject of royalty and tyranny. But there is a living interest about the speech delivered before Arcadius himself, which must be wanting in an imaginary dialogue between Alexander and Diogenes.

Synesius began[1] by disclaiming any intention of using the arts of rhetoric and poetry for the purpose of flattering the emperor and his friends. His desire is to bring back the long-exiled philosophy which, not content with expressing a qualified disapproval of some things about the palace and the court life, demands that searching criticism which pierces beneath the surface, and inflicts pain on the inmost heart. He will not belong to the class of those who mix poisonous drugs in sweet compounds, or who try by confectionery to tickle the appetite of the sick man ;[2] but to those who try to give and preserve health by

[1] "De Regno."   [2] Metaphor from Plato's "Gorgias."

the arts of medecine and training. His counsels will
be like salt, which stings while it preserves ; for the
life of a young and irresponsible ruler needs some
such constraining force. The city which has sent
him to present the suppliant's crown to the emperor,
and which will in gratitude decree another to him if he
will restore her to her primitive greatness, has also
commissioned him to make an offering of good advice.
He will proceed to his task, and show what things
should be sought and what eschewed by a monarch,
and if his hearer is conscious of having preferred the
evil course, may he feel a wholesome shame.

Synesius goes on to say that he appreciates the
wealth and strength of the empire without regarding
them as matter for praise. Wisdom is needed to
retain what fortune gives. Fortune may be a conse-
quence of good conduct, but the converse does not
hold. Arcadius should remember his father, whose
glorious life and success were a result of good
conduct, and should consider himself bound for that
reason to follow in his father's steps. The magnificence
on account of which his courtiers flatter him, is
common to kings who live for their people and
according to law, and to tyrants who live for themselves and bend all law to their will. A young ruler
who has inherited his dominion, needs most especially
the Divine guidance, but if he makes his will follow
wisdom and if fortune follow his will, he is in a
singularly happy position. Strength and understanding, either of which is insufficient by itself, should be
united in his person—a union symbolised by the
Egyptians in the figure of the Sphinx, and in the

twofold form of the god Hermes, who is represented as a young man standing beside an elder. But external goods, such as riches and power, are, as Plato, Aristotle, and later philosophers say, of the nature of tools, and we should pray that we may see them only in the possession of those who use them for good purposes, keeping guard over the people committed to them, and imitating, in their own sphere, the Divine Providence which should be symbolised in the life of a good king. For a king has a right to consider himself as governor of men in the same sense as that in which God is said to govern them, but only on condition that to the divine attribute of royalty he adds that of watchful care. For all the names by which men call God are relative, and pertain not to his nature in itself, but to their relations to him. So that when men agree in calling him good, they mean that they derive all good things from Him. And thus, so far as it is within their power, should kings be dispensers of good to all their subjects.

Continuing his description of the ideal monarch, Synesius lays down that piety is the foundation of all true kingship. Then, passing to the Platonic simile of the man and the many-headed animal dwelling together, he [1] shows how a king, above all other men, should be able to govern his own passions and appetites, and to maintain serenity while all the various parts of his nature work harmoniously together. Proceeding outwards, he considers the

---

[1] He omits the lion, but quotes a verse from the Medea in which the power of θυμός is shown.

immediate circle of a king's friends who should be friends not in name alone, and not subject to capricious treatment. No man is self-sufficient. A king who uses his friends well multiplies his powers of seeing, hearing, and judging. But the greatest possible care is necessary to keep flattery from gliding in under the mask of friendship, especially when the king, like Cyrus and Agesilaus, is generously suscep-tible to friendly attachment. From friends he pro-ceeds to discuss the soldiers who defend the State. The monarch should exercise with them in the field—the applause of bystanders will make the matter easy—and he should make use of all oppor-tunities of getting acquainted with the chief men among them. Soldiers, like the watch-dogs to whom Plato compares them, are apt to regard strangers as enemies. The emperor should not be a stranger to his men, but should be able both to call them by name, and, according to the advice given by Aga-memnon to Menelaus, exhort them to remember their own deeds and those of their fathers,[1] and should inspire enthusiasm by well-timed praise. Soldiers are his instruments, whom he should know as the shoemaker knows the quality of his leather and tools.

This leads to a strong declamation against those flatterers who try to make the monarch inaccessible and invisible; who seem to place him above all other men while they really debase him below them; who banish good sense from the precincts of the

---

[1] Rather an impossible task, one would suppose; but perhaps Synesius was thinking only of the Praetorian cohort.

palace, and whose influence undermines the manly
virtues by which alone a great empire has ever been
sustained. If the emperor will compare past times
with present, he will see that formerly, when the
leaders of men exposed themselves to the weather
and to the public gaze, barbarous nations were
subdued and taught to keep on the defensive. But
now that princes hide themselves like lizards, fearing
to let the multitude see that they are but men, and
can only walk on sprinkled gold-dust, these same
barbarians, having changed name and nature, are
threatening the empire itself. To illustrate the
simple grandeur and power of some of the late
emperors, Synesius tells the story how one of them [1]
received the Parthian ambassadors, while dining on
pea soup, and threatened to make the Parthian land
as bare as his own bald head.

It is to be regarded as a proof of the good sense
of the Romans in matters political that they have
rejected the term *rex* and use that of *imperator*
instead.[2] The functions of an imperator are by no
means honorary. As to the fear of emperors lest
they should make themselves too common, it shows
a want of genuineness. The sunlight is not contemptible because it is common, nor were heroes
like Agesilaus and Epaminondas to be despised for
living in public and eating plain food.

Now a critical time has come for the State. But

[1] He says Carinus, but the story will not fit Carinus. Volkmann suggests Carus.

[2] Αὐτοκράτωρ for βασιλεύς. Apparently the title βασιλεύς
is only used in complimentary style.

God and the emperor may yet ward off the threatened
evil. To come to particulars: the emperor should
make himself conversant with the army, and it is
most important that the army should be composed
of *native* soldiers, not of barbarians, who are no more
to be trusted by the emperor than are tamed wolves
by the shepherd. But now the enemies of the
empire are encouraged to practise the use of arms,
and natives are excused. Causes of war are certain
to arise, and then the Romans must succumb as
women fighting with men. Synesius enlarges in-
dignantly on the absurdity of employing barbarians
in high magisterial and military offices. He points
to the fact that the Romans make slaves of the
Scyths who are servile by nature; yet slaves may
become formidable if armed, as is shown by the
example of Spartacus and Crixus. It was in his
unappreciated kindness that Theodosius suffered this
miserable race[1] which the Cimmerians and Amazons
had conquered of old, to settle within Roman territory, whither their kinsfolk have followed in hordes.
Now a new departure must be taken. They must be
either reduced to subjection, or utterly expelled by a
stronger Roman army headed by a young and active
emperor.

To come to peaceful duties : these can be best performed by a monarch who has made himself respected
in war. It is his duty to associate with both classes of
his people, the military and the peaceful; and in the

---

[1] Synesius persists in confusing the Goths and the Scyths,
and surpasses even his own inaccuracy in his statements as to
the history of these peoples.

case of those who dwell at a distance, he should use
all opportunities of learning their wants by means of
embassies, to which he should ever be accessible.
The king should select his soldiers, and keep them
in discipline, lest the watch-dogs, after driving away
the wolves, should devour the flock, instead of being
content with their portion of milk. He should
live economically and so escape the necessity of
levying oppressive taxes. Avarice is worse in a king
than in a small dealer, who has at least the excuse
of the need to ward off poverty from his family.
Avaricious people put things in the contrary order
from the natural,—they make the soul exist for the
body and the body for external goods, instead of the
reverse. The king should conduct competitions in
wisdom and virtue, as those at Olympia, that he may
test and reward physical prowess. So will the golden
age return, the king leading the people in all things,
especially in public worship, himself favoured of God,
and wise in executing those functions in which, to
the people, he represents the Divine authority. Bene-
ficence, liberality, mercy, are to be the attributes of
the king, as they are of God, and to complete our
image of the ideal monarch, he must do good
naturally and without trouble, as the sun shines and
calls forth life by his own nature. He must rule
cosmically among the different grades of his depen-
dents, who are to take their appointed share in promoting the general well-being.

Synesius goes on to show the care that should
be taken in the appointment of governors and of
judges. As the emperor cannot carry on the whole

government by himself, he should act by means of a
few who are kept well in hand, as God governs the
world by the hand of nature. The best, not the
wealthiest, should be appointed to office. Rich and
rapacious men are apt to be remiss, and to condone
and to give confidence to greedy and mercenary
administrators and publicans. Thus may the influence of royalty make a change in the ideals and
characters of the people, and help them to estimate
all things according to their real worth.

Synesius concludes with an appeal to the emperor
on behalf of philosophy. There are many rivals with
her for his affections, and the divine flame is liable
to be extinguished so that it can never be rekindled.
Philosophy, indeed, does not need the praise of men,
for her dwelling is with God, but men need her help
for the prosperity of their affairs. Let the emperor
fulfil the dream of Plato, and bring philosophy into
union with monarchy. The promised sketch of the
ideal ruler is complete. May the shadow to which
it is reduced in words, give place to a living representation in the life of the emperor. And let the
first act of philosophical monarchy be to attend to
the grievances of these cities whose cause the philosopher has come to plead.

Such, in meagre outline, is the oration of Synesius,
" De Regno." It is impossible within our limits to
do justice to its elegance of style and the felicity of
expressions,[1] but even the above sketch shows the
remarkable boldness of the orator, which in later

---

[1] Readers unacquainted with Greek will find a most pleasing
German version in Krabinger's translation.

days he directly attributed to divine encouragement.[1]
We are also struck by the hopefulness of his temperament. He believed, apparently, that the young
emperor might actually take heed to his words, and
that if he would, he might yet restore both the entire
empire and the city of Cyrene to their former prosperity. In later days, instructed by bitter experience,
the utmost that he hoped for was that their inevitable
fate might be delayed.[2] And it is a noticeable sign
of the times that, in a speech so manly and independent in tone, we have so completely autocratic a
theory of government, and no hint of a right on the
part of subjects to manage their own affairs.

It was probably after the delivery of this oration
that Synesius saw the banishment of his friend
Aurelian and the entry of the Goths into Constantinople. As he was a personal witness of the exciting
events of those two years, we might expect that any
testimony from him would be of exceptional value.
Unfortunately, however, for the political historian,
though fortunately, perhaps, for the student of character and thought, he threw his experiences of events
into an allegorical form, under which he desired to
convey rather his own beliefs as to the method of
the divine government and the temporary success,
but final failure of evil principles, than any accurate
narrative of what actually took place. In the fable,
" De Providentia," he describes the fortunes of the
two brothers, Osiris and Typho, who, in Egyptian
mythology, represented the rival powers of light and

---

[1] " De Insomniis," c. ix.   [2] Ep. 73.

darkness. He makes Osiris a wise and good prince, chosen by the Egyptians to be their king. His wicked brother, Typho, prevails against him, with the help of the Scythian captain of the guards, and Osiris voluntarily gives himself up for the people, and goes into exile. Typho and the barbarians have their own evil way for a time. No laws are respected. The old regulations as to religious rites are relaxed in favour of the barbarians. Meantime, an unmannerly philosopher, who had come on an embassy to the city, is comforted by prognostications of better days to come. At last Providence intervenes on behalf of all the unhappy Egyptians. A sudden panic seizes the Scyths. Typho is defeated, and then accused of all his crimes, by the Egyptians, who sentence him to death, to which the gods add the pangs of Tartarus. Osiris returns in triumph, and brings back the Golden Age to men.

The philosophical purport of this story is clear, and will greatly help us when we come to consider the religious and cosmological views of Synesius. But thoroughly to sift out the historical from the allegorical portion is a task which can hardly be said to have been, as yet, satisfactorily performed. The explanatory preface and the concluding remarks of Synesius rather add to our embarrassment than relieve it. Certain analogies lie on the surface. Others are easy to conjecture, but hard to prove. Several indications point to Aurelian as the original of the character of Osiris, but what is said of Typho will not agree with what we know of Eutropius or Gainas, or any other of the mischief-makers at that crisis. But German scholarship seems to build on too slender foundations when it concludes, from certain points in this story, that Aurelian had a wicked brother[1] who was his own evil genius and that of the Eastern Empire. Such a person could hardly have escaped mention in some of the histories. But the entanglement is too great to be unravelled in this place.

However these things may have been, there can be little doubt that when Aurelian was banished Synesius lost his most influential friend at Constantinople. As he saw that he had no chance of success without the help of some persons about the court, he made an attempt to gain the favour of a certain Paeonius, for whom, as he was a person of culture, Synesius felt sufficient respect to be able to address him in very laudatory terms without incurring the charge of excessive flattery. For this man Synesius made out a plan of the heavens, apparently on a projection of his own invention,[2] with elaborate divisions into degrees, and representations of the inclination of the equator to the ecliptic, and verses inscribed on portions where there were no stars to be represented.

Modern men of science would smile at the opinion expressed by Synesius, that in his day science had advanced beyond its earliest stages, and could afford

---

[1] See the elaborate theory of Volkmann, "Synesius von Cyrene," ch. iii., of Aurelian's supposed brother. Also a full note in Neander's "Leben des heiligen Joh. Chrysostom." See also a note on Aurelian in vol. v. of Tillemont's "Histoire des Empereurs."

[2] "De Dono Astrolabii," Ep. 153.

to regard the ornamental as well as the merely useful. But, whatever the quality of his amateur work, it pleased Paeonius sufficiently to induce him to do what he could for Synesius. It was not, however, till after the return of Aurelian that his business was settled, and he himself able to go back to Cyrene. The actual results of the negotiations are not known. From statements he made afterwards, it seems that he had achieved something, but the good done cannot have been permanent. The manner of his departure at last was very sudden and unexpected. Constantinople experienced, as seems to have been not unfrequently the case, a violent shock of earthquake. There was a general scare in the city, which had the effect, as we know from the homilies of Chrysostom, as well as from the letters of Synesius, of sending the panic-stricken people to the churches in a fit of tardy and ephemeral penitence. Synesius, thinking, as he said, that the sea was under such circumstances a safer place than the land, hastily embarked in a ship that he found in dock, and sailed off without saying good-bye to his friends, or making the promised gift of the rug, an act of negligence for which he afterwards sent sufficient apologies. He had not, probably, with him the wherewithal to pay his heavier debts, which he afterwards scrupulously discharged through his friend Pylaemenes. He seems to have touched first at Alexandria, and then to have taken ship again to Cyrene; for we have reason to assign to this period a most pleasing and racy letter, describing the perils of his homeward voyage. The captain was a man en-cumbered with debt, who would rather have preferred

death to life ; the helmsman a fanatical Jew, who would
have thought it a meritorious act to send as many
Gentiles as possible to the bottom of the sea. The
ship twice was run aground, and then carried away
almost out of sight of land ; and when the passengers
remonstrated, the captain complained that they were
unreasonable people to grumble and be afraid both of
land and of sea. Presently, the wind rose and turned
the sail right round, at which the captain only growled
that it was not an easy thing to sail scientifically. But
the situation became worse when the sun set on Friday
evening, and the Jewish helmsman threw himself
prone on deck, and refused to break the Sabbath by
continuing his work in steering. No entreaties nor
threats could move him till near midnight, when he
suddenly jumped up, saying, "Now the law allows it
because we are in peril of our lives," and recommenced
his work. The plight of their ship grew more desperate as the storm rose. At length they came near
the shore, and a friendly man of the country came on
board and helped them to land ; after which their
only danger was from want of provisions, till these
were supplied by the hospitable kindness of the barbarous people of the coasts.

Much might be written about the probable effect
on the mind of Synesius of his stay in Constantinople.
The letter above quoted proves, by his lively, and, in
parts, almost flippant tone, that his spirit was not
broken, nor his sense of honour blunted by his adversities. His mental attitude towards Christian doctrine and Christian society was, probably, not much
altered. He must have been brought into contact

with more Christian people than he had known at
Alexandria. Aurelian, himself, seems to have been a
munificent builder of churches,[1] as well as an intimate
friend of John Chrysostom.. One would have liked
to believe that Synesius came into contact with Chrysostom himself, and derived from him a very different
idea of Christian life from any that he could have
obtained from Theophilus. The philosopher and the
saint would have had much in common in their hatred
of social and political corruption, and their desire to
return to simple and rational modes of life. But
Chrysostom was not a man likely to cultivate the
acquaintance of Synesius. His noble nature was de-
fective just where that of Synesius was most excellent
—in geniality and flexibility. He never dined in
company, and had no taste for social life. He is only
once named in the letters of Synesius, and then with
an insignificant though laudatory epithet. The hymn
of thanksgiving which Synesius composed on his
return home is thoroughly Neo-Platonic, and not distinctly Christian. True, he says in it that he had wept
and prayed much in many sacred places in Thrace,
but it seems quite consistent with the character of
Synesius, that he should have worshipped in Christian
temples,—generally, at that time, kept open for
private prayer,—simply because those of the Pagans
were shut up ; and he certainly regarded the martyrs at
whose shrines the churches were built, as the tutelary

---

[1] See note in Tillemont, vol. v. I am inclined to think that
Aurelian was baptized during his exile, else the expressions in
"De Providentia" about the initiation of Osiris (bk. ii., ch. 5)
seem rather futile.

deities of the land. One sentence in the " De Regno " would conclusively prove that he was acquainted with the customs of Christians, and even with their communion service ;[1] but the text is here hopelessly corrupt. We can, however, affirm with certainty, that at this period Synesius had arrived at those convictions which, with a few modifications, he held to the end of his life ; and that he regarded absolute truth as incapable of being fully expressed in any religion whatsoever, but as shadowed forth in many symbolical forms, and discernible only to the heart purified from passions, and the mind intent on contemplation.

[1] The allusion in ch. v. to the prayer "in the mysteries." The suggestion in Petavius, followed by Krabinger, would give a clear sense to an otherwise very obscure passage. But it is highly improbable that, whether a Christian or not, Synesius had before this time been baptized.

CHAPTER III.

SYNESIUS AS COUNTRY GENTLEMAN.

'Εμοὶ μὲν οὖν βίος βιβλία καὶ θήρα.[1]
"Ἵνα γὰρ ὑγιαίνῃ ψυχή τε καῖ σῶμα, τὸ μέν τι δεῖ ποιεῖν, τὸ δὲ αἰτεῖν τὸν Θεόν.[2]

WHEN we are studying the history of any period of marked political decline—such as is generally both cause and effect of a similar decline in moral tone and in material prosperity—when the mind is wearied with the pettiness and the intrigues which determine the gravest affairs, and the heart is sick with tales of cruelty, perfidy, and relentless oppression, there is some consolation in the thought that there are, after all, some spheres of life which are more or less removed from the blighting influence of a weak or vicious government, some sources of human happiness which bad regulations may check but cannot entirely stop, some regions where the recuperative forces of nature can at least make a stand against the desolating ravages of man. The historian looks principally at capitals and at persons and places most immediately affected by political events. Remote country regions force themselves into notice only when their sufferings have led them to cry for redress.

---

[1] Synesius, "De Insomniis," c. ix.   [2] Ep. 57.

And, doubtless, times like those of the dying empire
were full of misery both to the near and to the
distant subjects of the incapable despot. Yet, even
in such times, in the intervals of actual invasions or
extraordinary seasons of distress, to people who can
keep out of law-suits, and can manage to pay their
taxes, some of the commonest and the best joys of
life are not wanting. Agriculture affords healthful
toil and a reward to the diligent husbandman ; the
chase maintains the vigour of those who rejoice in
abundant physical energy. The scholar may forget
present troubles in the society of the great men of
the past, and the poet delight in the ever-fresh
beauties of Nature. The mutual affection of husband
and wife, of parents and children, of congenial friends
and fellow-students, lightens labour and brightens
sport. Country people enjoy their simple games, and
festivals, and stories round the winter fire. Religious
worship lifts rich and poor alike above the distractions
of present cares. Civic life may perish utterly ; but
there are two kinds of life far less easy to destroy—
that of the high-souled thinker who is raised above
the ordinary course of human affairs, and that of the
simple countryman who has never risen to higher
desires than the satisfaction of the commonest needs
of man.

Thus, we must not think it a strange thing that the
quiet years of private life, which intervened between
the embassy of Synesius to Constantinople and his
elevation to the episcopate of Ptolemais, were, in
spite of the wretched state of public affairs, of wars
and rumours of wars, of distress and rapine, a time

which afterwards seemed to him to have been full of
peace and happiness.[1] Doubtless the cares of responsibility in after years made the time of freedom
seem delightful in comparison.   But the pleasures of
a rural domestic life were not, for Synesius, a blessing
unappreciated till withdrawn.   He was of a happy
temperament, ready to accept thankfully all the good
things that he met in the course of his ordinary life,
and to find amusement in the ludicrous side of what
was painful.[2]   And his tedious stay in Thrace ha l
made him all the more capable of enjoying his
beautiful native land, and the society of his early
friends.

Synesius seems to have spent a considerable part
of his time on a country estate, probably inherited
from his father, in the southern part of the province,
near to the salt-pits of Ammon.   Several of his
letters, however, must have been written from Cyrene
or the neighbourhood, and a few from Alexandria.
He also made a journey to Greece, but probably did
not stay there long.   With his strong affections and
domestic tastes, he was not likely to be long un-
married, and his marriage may be with considerable
probability assiged to the year 403 A.D.,[3] three years
after his return from Constantinople.   His wife was
an Alexandrian lady, and must have been a Christian,
for the marriage ceremony was performed by the

[1] See especially letter 57.

[2] For his sense of humour under painful circumstances, see
especially his letters 4. 67, and 104.

[3] He mentions his wife and *one* babe in the only letter in
which he gives the consul of the year (404).

Bishop Theophilus himself.[1] The marriage seems to
have been a happy one. Synesius was evidently
much attached to his wife. She is mentioned very
affectionately in one of his hymns.[2] When he is
preparing for battle, it is only the thought of her and
of their babe that can make him shrink from death.
We shall see hereafter his determination not to give
her up on his adopting the clerical life. Yet she
cannot have been a woman of very strong character
or of intellectual tastes, for, in all the numerous
letters of Synesius, she is hardly ever mentioned, and
then but casually, though at that time and especially
in that country, women were not compelled to a life
of entire seclusion, but were able to obtain a good
education, and sometimes a position of influence.[3]
To him she was, before all things, the mother of his
children, and that seems to be the only capacity in
which he habitually regarded her.

The children of Synesius were a source to him of
intense pride and delight. He welcomed them into
the world with an exultation that makes his untimely
loss of them in the latter part of his life the more
pathetic. He went so far as to dedicate a book[4] to
an expected son. Some of his children were born at

---

[1] Ep. 105.   [2] Hymn 8.

[3] The Cyreneans were Dorians, and women in Dorian states
were much freer than in Ionian. Herodotus tells the story of
Queen Pheretima, who upheld her son's cause against the
Persians. Arete, daughter of Aristippus, was a female philosopher of Cyrene. It is a curious fact, however, that in "De
Providentia," in describing the wife of Osiris, Synesius seems
to advocate female seclusion. Is he here making personal allusions?   [4] The "Dion.'

Alexandria,[1] and this seemed to give him an additional tie to that city. Besides his own three boys, Synesius had for a time a young son of Euoptius, Dioscurius by name, living under his charge. He took considerable interest in this boy's education, and saw that he learned to repeat fluently fifty lines of poetry every day.[2] He was anxious that his children should early become fond of books, because he regarded general literature as an almost necessary preliminary to severer studies ; yet he did not overrate the educational value of book-learning, but considered that the chief use of books was to stimulate the mental faculties,[3] not merely to supply a fund of facts. Besides his little nephew, Synesius had at one time a niece staying with him, probably a daughter of Stratonice,[4] and he was so fond of her as to lament loudly when her other uncle, Euoptius, sent for her to come to him. Euoptius himself was living during part of this time at Phycus, the port of Cyrene, so that when Synesius was in the city the brothers were within an easy drive of one another (or even within a walk, if the household of Synesius had not strongly remonstrated with him on the impropriety of taking the journey on foot, and even forced him to stay at home by taking away his coat [5]), and Euoptius was

---

[1] Ep. 18.
[2] Ep. 53, 111.
[3] " Dion," ch. xv.
[4] Ep. 56. Or of another sister. I am inclined to think that one of the sisters of Synesius died young, as only one is mentioned in Hymn 8. Yet in Ep. 144 he mentions his niece as the daughter of Amelius (or perhaps Stratonice was twice married).
[5] Ep. 109. I should have been inclined to think that this

E

able to send his brother vegetables (especially
silphium)[1] from his kitchen garden.[2]

The care of a household involved the supervision
of a number of slaves. Synesius experienced some
little trouble in this respect, but seems to have been
a kind, easy-going master. When one of his slaves
ran away, and he had to ask his friend Herculianus
to help to get him back, he explained that this slave
had not been bred in his own household, or he would
not have ran away. His own servants were treated
by him almost as equals, and they loved him more
than they feared him. He would have preferred to
let him go, rather than to acknowledge that " the
worse do not depend upon their betters, but those
who profess to be better on the worse ;" but the man
belonged to his niece, and he could not expect her to
take the same view of the matter.[3] On another
occasion, he had to ask Euoptius to help him to get
rid of a slave whom he had bought for a trainer, but
who had proved an incorrigible drunkard. The man
is not to be punished (since vice is its own punishment) otherwise than by being sent home to his own
country ; but on his journey he must be kept from
the wine-jars, and bound, as Odysseus when passing
the Sirens, lest he should tempt the sailors to drink.

letter was written after Synesius had been made bishop, but
that he asks for news from Ptolemais (later the seat of his
bishopric), and also that Euoptius afterwards removed to
Alexandria.   •

    [1] One of the chief products of Cyrene.   See the coin on
title-page.
    [2] Ep. 106.   [3] Ep. 144.

Synesius was able to indulge his social temperament by having frequent visitors to stay in his house; but it is probable that more came to see him when he was in Cyrene than ever found their way to him on his lonely farm. There, however, he was able to derive considerable amusement from his observation of the ways of the country people. They were, he said, quite antediluvian in their habits.[1] They had never seen fish till he showed them a barrel of salt fish from Egypt, which quite frightened them, as they could not believe that the water, which, in a pure form, they only knew in wells, produced anything edible. Their music was simple enough for Plato's Republic. They knew nothing of kings and courtiers and changes of fortune. They knew of the continued existence of the emperor,—the presence of the tax-gatherer was a perpetual witness to that fact,—but they had some notion that his name was Agamemnon, of whom, one suspects, Synesius himself had told them stories, and that he had a friend, Odysseus, who had had, a short time back, amusing adventures with Polyphemus. He was evidently on friendly terms with them, and we would much like to know what they thought of him.

Synesius seems to have had much of that genuine appreciation of the simple sights and sounds of nature, which is far more frequently found in modern than in ancient times, and which, perhaps, cannot be felt by men who have not been for a time hampered by the conditions of life in a large city. His liberty··

---

[1] Ep. 147.

loving nature delighted in freedom from constraint.
When he thought of the work of advocates, whose
time was measured by a water-clock; or of rhetoricians
who trembled before their audience, dreading the
criticism of the attentive listener, and angry at the
inattention of the careless ; or of teachers, who had
to make their time and opportunities wait upon their
pupils, and to load their memories with book-lore,
instead of using their critical faculty on the books
they read, he contrasted his own happier position.
There was no necessity for him to trouble himself
about pupils or hearers.   Living in the country, with
himself for his only audience, he had for water-clock
the ever-flowing stream, and the cypress-trees for his
only public.[1]   The sunlight was to him the most
blessed of all sights ; the hum of the bees the sweetest
music.[2]   And he had deeper reasons than mere fancies
for preferring a quiet and somewhat lonely life.   We
shall see, later on, how, all through his life, he felt
that his impetuous and easily-distracted mind needed
seasons of perfect calm and tranquillity, in which he
could collect his thoughts, and realize, in the operations of nature and in his own mind, that Divine
Presence which was, for him, so easily obscured by
the distracting cares of a life without leisure.[3]

The chief occupations of Synesius in his country
life were agriculture, hunting, military exercises, reading, and writing.   He felt himself something of an
amateur at farming, and confessed that he increased

---

[1] "Dion," ch. xi., xii.   [2] Ep. 147.
[3] See Hymn III., composed on a pilgrimage in the interior of
Libya.

no part of his patrimony except that which consisted
of books. But he lived in a fertile country, and was
able to raise barley, which supplied them with a drink
as well as with food, olives, heavy for exportation, but
good for lamps, grapes, figs, and honey second only
to that of Hymettus. But the chief wealth of the
farmers in the Pentapolis was in live-stock. They
possessed large herds of cattle, goats (whose milk
they preferred to that of cows), camels, and mares.
Synesius took especial intesest in the breeding of
horses. In sending one to a friend,[1] he remarked
that the horses of his country were rather bony, and
that this particular one, though useful for hunting,
races, processions, or military operations, was rather
ugly about the head ; but with horses as with men,
the gifts of nature are not all accumulated on one.
Synesius took an intense pleasure in the chase. He
wrote a book about hunting, which has not come
down to us. One of the animals hunted was the
ostrich,[2] which seems, however, not to have been
bred. He also occupied himself with military exercises, and seems to have been something of a con-
noisseur of arms. We shall see that there was a great
diversity among the weapons used in actual warfare
by the people among whom he lived, and he probably
acquired skill in the use of many of them.

But his active pursuits were, after all, not so delightful to him as his books. We may distinguish
two kinds of reading which occupied his leisure time.
On the one hand, he read a great deal of what he

---

[1] Ep. 40. [2] Ep. 133.

considered to belong to philosophy proper. And, at
the same time, he amused his lighter moments and
stored his mind with illustrations by reading widely
throughout the field of Greek literature. It has been
concluded,[1] from the awkward way in which he
Hellenises Latin words, that he had no acquaintance
with Latin literature. But with the Greek poets and
orators of all periods and all styles he seems to have
been familiar. His own feeling in regard to letters
is gracefully expressed in his work " Dion."[2] All
Greeks, he says, who have written anything good, of
any sort, are to be had in honour. Literature trains
us from childhood—when philosophy would be too
strong medicine for us—till we can rise to further
heights, and when we have attained them, and are
weary with the exertion, we give ourselves up once
more to Calliope, and she soothes and restores us
for fresh efforts. Nor are poetry and rhetoric useless
to a man who delights in them for their own sake,
without a desire for high philosophy, for such men
are gratified and improved by culture, and are not
to be wholly despised. In the realms of the air
there is room for singing birds, as well as for eagles.

Midway between his light reading and his abstruse
speculations, we should place the studies of Synesius
in mathematics and in natural science. We have
already seen that he took great interest in astronomy
and in hydrostatics, and he seems to have had a
slight acquaintance with some writers on medicine.[3]
But, along with his literary tastes, Synesius was sin-

---

[1] By Clausen.   [2] Ch. x.   [3] Ep. 115.

gularly loose in his method both of reading and of
writing. In both occupations we seem to see the
effects of his want of intellectual companionship, and
his exaggerated fear of becoming a slave to the letter,
instead of penetrating to the inner meaning of the
authors he read. He says[1] that in reading, whether
to himself or to others, he would occasionally withdraw his eyes from the book, and finish a sentence
for himself, thus using a test to show whether he had
caught the spirit of the author, and acquiring a useful
facility in dealing with corrupt texts. He despised
the tinkering up of manuscripts, and held in abhorrence the habit of calling up authorities to prove any
point. To his freedom in dealing with all the books
he read, he owed that freshness and vigour which is
the great charm of his writings, and that want of
accuracy, and sometimes of moderation, which is
their chief defect.

During this period of his life, Synesius was a
prolific and very miscellaneous writer. Besides the
lost " Cynegetica "[2] already mentioned, and perhaps
the latter portion of his " De Providentia," he wrote,
during this time, three treatises—" De Insomniis "
(" Concerning Dreams "), " Calvitæ Encomium "
(" Praise of Baldness "), and " Dion "—a quantity of
poetry, of which only a part has come down to us,
and letters innumerable, chiefly to friends in Constantinople or in Alexandria. These letters are to
be included among his literary compositions, for
though in many of them he writes in a free, un-

---

[1] " Dion," ch. xvi.   [2] Ep. 153.

premeditated manner, he evidently took pains with
their style, so as to make them fit to be read to
others besides those to whom they were immediately
addressed. He cultivated the elegant art of saying
uninteresting things in an interesting way; and in
ordering a coat,[1] or introducing a friend, or inviting
a guest, he relieved the triviality of the matter by
lively touches and unexpected turns of expression.
In return, he always awaited eagerly the letters of
his friends, and sometimes wrote in a rather captious
tone of discontent when they had shown negligence
in correspondence.

Of his treatises, that "Concerning Dreams," though
a very hasty composition, is interesting in that it sets
forth his views as to the forces of nature and the
perceptions of man. The "Praise of Baldness" is
a curious example of the rhetorical style in vogue in
his day, and certainly laid him open to the adverse
criticisms of those who objected to his blending
jest with earnest, and wasting the powers of his
mind on trivial subjects. Regarded as a *jeu d'esprit*,
it is ingenious and amusing. It may be thought a
difficult matter to bring forward at least seventeen
arguments—scientific, metaphysical, and historical—
to prove that it is better to be bald than to have a
good head of hair, but Synesius, who seems to have
lost his own hair early, had been reading Dion
Chrysostom's "Praise of Hair," and was determined
to make the most of the opposite cause against
his favourite orator. He may seem to have some

---

[1] Ep. 52.

show of reason on his side, when he mentions
the thickness of skull found in bald-headed races,
and the advantage in most diseases of shaving the
head. But his arguments seem weaker when he
points to the stupidity of the most hairy or woolly
animals, and to the customary inferiority of men
to women in length of hair. He is more fanciful
still when he points to the steadfastness of the round
stars and the inconstancy of the hairy comets; or
when he argues that, as a flower sheds its useless,
but showy petals before the fruit can ripen, so must
a man shed his hair before his brain can fulfil its
proper functions. But he is most sophistical when
he tries to explain away Homer's references to the
long-haired Achæans, and to prove that Hector was
bald, and that Achilles may have had no hair except
on the back of his head !

Whether this work was composed before or after
the "Dion," the style of thinking and of writing which
belongs to it is such as to provoke the kind of censure against which, in that latter work, Synesius drew
up an apology. The grounds on which he was
attacked, and his method of defence and retaliation,
are set forth in a very interesting letter to Hypatia.[1]
His hostile critics, he says, are of two kinds, stern
ascetics, probably monks of Christian and of pre-
Christian sects,—for both were to be found in his
neighbourhood,—disapproved the lightness of his
style, and his fondness for profane literature, requiring
him to be, like themselves, always full of theolo-

---

[1] Ep. 153. See "Dion," *passim*.

gical disputations, in season and out of season; whereas such arguments seemed to him a presumptuous attempt to fathom the infinite, and an impious profanation of the sacred mysteries. On the other hand, would-be learned, little-minded sophists objected to his freedom of style and to his neglect of their rules and methods. In this treatise, accordingly, he vindicates, as we have seen, the recreative functions of light literature, and the superiority of liberal culture to pedantic scholarship. It also contains many interesting points illustrating his opinions on the true ideal of life, to which we shall recur when we come to examine his position in philosophy.

Of the poetry of Synesius, a great part must have perished. All that has come down to us consists of ten poems embodying his religious musings. One or two[1] of them probably belong to a later period, but others can with certainty be assigned to this.[2] They are generally pleasing and musical in diction, mystical and obscure in expression, and will help us more than any of his other writings to discern the way in which he gradually came to combine the Neo-Platonic theories he had learned from Hypatia, and the strong Hellenic sentiment of the later Polytheists, with the scheme of Christian doctrine and the tone of Christian feeling acquired in the course of his later life.

The quiet pursuits of these years, in the fields, the forest, and the library, were temporarily interrupted

---

[1] Probably only Hymn X.

[2] Thus Hymn III. was written just after his return from his embassy. In Hymn VIII. there is mention of his wife and of *two* children.

in three ways; by journeys, by interventions in the
law-courts, or with authorities on behalf of friends,
and, once at least, by a serious invasion of the enemy,
which called for strong efforts of national defence.
We have already mentioned his visits to Alexandria.
His journey to Greece was probably made not very
long after his return to Cyrenaica.[1] His motive in
going was, probably, mere curiosity. He told his
brother,[2] apparently in jest, that priests and other
friends had been trying to persuade him to go by
telling him dreams, which they called revelations.
He said he wanted to get away from his present
troubles, meaning possibly the vexation he felt at the
cowardice of the military governors, and his inability
to help. He adds, as a further reason, that he did
not like to be at a disadvantage with those travellers
who plumed themselves, though they might know less
than he did of philosophy, on having actually seen the
Academy, the Lyceum, and the Porch,—or, rather,
the place where the Porch used to be, for the pro-
consul[3] had had it removed. Accordingly, he went and
returned able to say that he had seen these places;
but he was not much gratified by his visit.[4] Nothing
great was left at Athens, except her old memories.
The land of Hypatia was far richer in philosophy, and
in everything else except honey. When we consider
that Alaric and his Goths had been in the country
within ten years of the visit of Synesius, and that the
ravages of the successive pro-consuls had probably
been worse than those of the barbarians, we need not

---

[1] Clausen thinks he cannot have been married at the time.

[2] Ep. 54.   [3] Of Achaia.   [4] Ep. 135.

wonder if the philosopher felt as keen a disappointment with the city of Plato, as that of an enthusiastic
mediæval monk on his first pilgrimage to Rome.

The interventions of Synesius in public affairs, were,
during this time, always made in a private capacity
and on behalf of individuals. He complains that
people will leave him no peace, but will be always
begging him to interfere on their account, though there
can be little doubt that, with his generous disposition
and rather fussy temperament, he really enjoyed such
opportunities of using influence. He probably used
his privilege as ex-delegate to be excused from the
tiresome duties of senator,[1] and he resisted the so-
licitations of his friend Herculianus, who offered his
influence to procure some public post for him.[2] But
in spite of his retirement, he felt obliged to come
forward for the public good, when he saw the shameful
corruption of the tribunals. Especially when a certain
Peter had been setting the laws at defiance, commit-
ting acts of fraud, and threatening the officers of
justice. Synesius seems to have brought about a
combination of notable men to uphold the authority of
the law, and he wrote to authorities at Constantinople
to prevent Peter from making a successful appeal.[3]
But the most curious and interesting case of his
efforts on behalf of justice, is that of a certain John,
who was accused of murder. There is evidently more
than one man of this name who figures in the letters

---

[1] Ep. 99.

[2] Epp. 143, 145. The circumstances are not quite clear.

[3] Ep. 47. But I do not see why Clausen thinks this letter
must have been written before Synesius was made bishop.

of Synesius ; but if we might take, as referring to one
person, all those passages respecting which we cannot
prove the contrary, we should have material for con-
structing a remarkable life of successful villany. Indeed, this man would seem to be the most troublesome
person, except one, with whom Synesius ever had to
deal. He has to write him sharp reprimands for
abusing his friendship with powerful persons,[1] for
making immoderate demands,[2] and for trying to bribe
the judges.[3] John had been accused of murdering a
certain Aemilius, and Synesius, writing to Euoptius,
expressed his belief that, whether the accusation were
true or false, John's character was such as to give
colour to it, and his disgust at being dragged into
interfering in such a miserable affair.[4] At the same
time, he wrote to John himself a very curious letter,[5]
couched in terms of studied, and perhaps ironical,
courtesy, yet expressing grave suspicions, and offering
very unwelcome advice. He urges John to give himself up to justice. So only, if he is guilty, can divine
and human punishment purge away his sin, before it
becomes entirely engrained in his nature ; or, if he is
innocent, can he be re-admitted into the society of
respectable people. He should also give up the
ruffian whom he is accused of having abetted, and
who is likely to confess the truth under torture.
John certainly does not seem to have availed himself
of the moral advantages which Synesius set before
him. It may have been before or after this that
he improved his position by currying favour with

---

[1] Ep. 63.   [2] Ep. 64.   [3] Ep. 2.
[4] Ep. 50.   Chronology very uncertain.   [5] Ep. 44.

Antiochus, the Persian resident at the Byzantine Court. Perhaps it was to escape his evil repute that he adopted for a time a monastic life, on which occasion Synesius addressed to him an ironical letter of congratulation.[1] But even then, he could not permanently be rid of him ; for he seems to have come from his retirement, and joined the evil crew that embittered the last years of Synesius.[2] Probably, however, none of his later actions made him so contemptible in the eyes of Synesius as did the arrant cowardice he had once shown when in a position of military authority.

The Pentapolis seems to have been in a chronic state of insecurity from the neighbouring Libyan tribes. The same year that Synesius returned from Constantinople, he found a good deal to occupy him in taking precautions against the enemy,[3] and he seems to have found a difficulty in sending the produce of his farm down to the coast. But four years later, in 404 A.D.,[4] the danger became more pressing, as a barbarous horde invaded the country, carried off the cattle, and laid siege to the strong places in which the country people took refuge— perhaps even to the city of Cyrene itself.[5] The

---

[1] Ep. 146. But, as there is no mention of penitence in that letter, I am inclined to think that it must have been addressed to some other John, and so was possibly not ironical.

[2] Ep. 50. [3] Ep. 61.

[4] Ep. 132. Date of Consuls Aristænetus and another (Honorius).

[5] Ep. 129. Clausen thinks, from the use of the word Κυρηναίοις in this letter, that it must have been written from Cyrene, but the writer would certainly seem to be in a place nearer the coast.

hostile tribes on this occasion were the Macetæ, who are called by similar names in the works of various authors, and are probably descended from the Macæ of Herodotus,[1] whom he places on the Greater Syrtis. Synesius was for some time confined in one of the strong places, and he wrote to his friend Olympius, in Seleucia, begging him to send arms, especially arrows, for the Syrian arrows were smoother and steadier in flight than any he could get from Egypt. He also asked for a good horse, named Italus, which had been promised to him, and which some cunning forger had tried to secure, by adding to the letter from Olympius a postscript to the effect that Italus must stay in Seleucia. But the efforts of private citizens were of little effect, while the generals showed utter incompetency and cowardice. On this occasion the *dux* Cerealius, who had been wringing money out of the cities while the enemy was devastating the country, had put all his treasures on board ship, and then embarked and attempted to direct the defensive operations by sending little boats, while he tried to impress upon the citizens that they had better not run the risk of an attack. Before this Cerealius had been made *dux*, a band of mounted archers called Balagritæ[2] had helped to defend the province, but now their horses had been taken away. Synesius was very active during the siege, and had at the same time to write letters of encouragement to his brother in Phycus, who seems not to have shared his martial ardour. We do not know what was the end of this

[1] Book IV., c. 175.
[2] Clausen suggests Bulgarians.

raid, but a little while afterwards we find Synesius collecting arms and raising recruits for an expedition to meet the enemy. He writes very martial letters to his brother. He would gladly die to restore peace and order to the city. He has been especially delighted in hearing of the valiant resistance to the enemy made by a body of rustic people, headed by their clergy,[1] in a narrow valley, and especially at the daring of a deacon named Faustus, who had killed a barbarian leader by knocking him on the head with a big stone. His Spartan blood was up. He thought of the words of the ephors to Leonidas and his men: "Fight as if doomed to die, and so you shall not die." The great traditions of the Roman Empire animated him likewise, and, though the Romans are not what they once were, he comforts himself with the proverb, that even a decrepit camel can bear a heavier load than many asses. He thinks, too, of all that is dear to him in his native land. These nomad brigands risk their lives for stolen goods ;—should the citizens venture nothing for what is their own?[2] He grows very impatient when the ravages become worse, the children being killed when captured, to save the trouble of guarding them; yet the citizens still sit at home, discussing the conduct and the pay of the soldiers, while he would rouse the whole country to arms.[3] He writes again from the field, in a host of motley-armed men, for whom he has procured lances,

---

[1] The mention of this valiant action of the clergy is more remarkable, if we understand the words ὅτι μὴ Κυρήβαντές εἰσι, &c., to refer to the priests, rather than to the enemy.

[2] Ep. 113. [3] Ep. 125.

two-edged swords, carved daggers, axes, clubs, and shields. A battle is expected in two days, and, should he fall, he begs Euoptius to take care of his children.[1] But the desired battle was never fought. When the soldiers, especially the Balagritæ, were ready to fight, the *dux* John, who seems to have been a worthy successor to Cerealius, suddenly disappeared, and rumours were set afloat that he had fallen ill, or had broken his leg, or that some other misfortune had happened to him. After some days, when the enemy seemed to have determined not to advance, he suddenly reappeared, in excellent health, and, with a good deal of brag and fussiness, prepared for an advance. He told them that he had been to succour some of their allies, for the mere rumours of his being among any people kept the enemy aloof. The army of defence marched on, but, as soon as they came in sight of a poor, seemingly famine-stricken band of the enemy, John set spurs to his horse, and galloped away in a style that did more credit to his horsemanship than to his valour, till he reached a mountain fastness, into which he could creep as a mouse into its hole. The army waited awhile, dis-heartened and distrustful. The enemy was prepared for defence, not for attack, and finally a retreat was made on both sides without a blow being struck.[2] What was the use of the patriotism and energy or the Dorian blood of a volunteer leader, when officials would not do their duty? The barbarians continued their periodical raids, but we do not know that they

---

[1] Ep. 108.   [2] Ep. 104.

made another wholesale irruption for some years. When the next season of peril came, Synesius was as anxious as ever about the fate of his country, but before that time he had changed the sword for the crozier.

It may seem paradoxical to regard a life like this as one of peace and quietness; but, as we have already said, it afforded intervals of leisure, during which, in the healthful pursuits of hunting and of agriculture, amid the pleasures of domestic life, Synesius could forget for a time the dangers of hostile inroads and the vexations of tyrannical officials; and thus he could immerse himself in those philosophical studies, the results of which, to his mind and character, we must study in order to understand his claim to the title by which he preferred to call himself, Synesius the Philosopher.

CHAPTER IV.

SYNESIUS AS PHILOSOPHER.

Οὐ γὰρ ἀπόχρη μὴ κακὸν εἶναι, ἀλλὰ δεῖ καὶ Θεὸν εἶναι.[1]

Φιλοσοφίας λεγούσης τοὺς θεοὺς οὐδὲν ἄλλο ἢ ῥοῖς.[2]

ALL the terms used by man to denote his mental faculties and the various fields in which those faculties are exercised change their meaning from age to age, as by fresh accumulations of experience or the opening up of new regions to mental enterprise, he is led to change his point of view in regarding both the world around him and the world within. Thus, the term which stands, or should stand, for the highest kind of human knowledge has not always been uniform in signification. If we would understand what the word Philosophy meant to thinkers of the fourth and fifth centuries, and especially to Synesius himself,—and, unless we do in some measure understand it, we cannot possibly enter into his whole manner of thinking and living,—we must strip that term of some of the associations which it has acquired from the supercilious materialism of the last century, and add to it much that is now comprised in the ordinary conception of religion. But

---

[1] Synesius, " Dion," c. viii.   [2] " De Insomniis," c. i.

in spite of many shiftings of sense, we shall perhaps
find that both then and now and through the intermediate time, the word, when carefully used, has
corresponded to one fundamental idea—the search
for unity. Regarded on its theoretical or speculative
side, philosophy seeks, and in some measure attains,
a standpoint from which the mind can view all things
presented to its consciousness in relation to itself and
to one another. While each separate science traces
such relations in one restricted field, philosophy
binds together the partial systems as fast as they
are constructed, and reserves a place for such as are
yet to be made. But since a perfectly-comprehensive
and self-consistent scheme of philosophy seems to
be beyond the scope of human invention, we may
fittingly regard as of the nature of philosophy that
whole region of thought which supplies the combining
and harmonising principles of knowledge. Again,
philosophy is always regarded as having a practical as
well as a speculative side; and here, too, her aim is
unity—the establishment of such principles as shall
give consistency to the whole course of action, and
bring about a harmony among motives and efforts.
Such principles must, of course, be derived from
theory, though their practical cogency does not
always depend upon logical sequence. With schools
and with individuals, speculative and practical principles seem often not to be interdependent, but to be
mutually dependent on a particular tone of mind or a
particular degree of mental and moral energy. But
the genuine thinker will always accept, in their highest
and broadest sense, the words of Descartes, whose aim

in devising his system was—"to discriminate the false from the true, so as to see clearly in action, and to walk sure-footedly in this life." For rational discrimination involves a clear idea as to what constitutes truth and falsity, and no walking can be sure-footed that is not directed towards a single goal.

In most of the systems of the declining years of Greek philosophy, the practical element decidedly prevailed over the speculative. It has often been observed that the systems of the Stoics, the Epicureans, and the Cynics were more of the nature of religion than of what we commonly regard as philosophy, — that they aimed, in the first place, at a consistent rule of life, and but secondarily at an explanation of the universe. It might seem at first sight that this remark will not apply to the Alexandrian school, with its vague though glorious speculations, and its attempts to rise from all mundane considerations to the regions of pure thought. But a slight study of the Neo-Platonists convinces us that their fundamental character was intensely practical. Their doctrine of the universe and of the soul formed the basis for a strict system of self-discipline, which many practised with assiduity. They cannot be said to have placed knowledge above conduct, for with them conduct was not three-fourths, nor any definite proportion of life, but embraced the whole, pure thought being itself considered an act of the highest type, and the power of contemplation as the very noblest of human energies. Besides its practical nature, another peculiarity of the latest Greek philosophy was its catholicity, its eagerness to reach

beyond the special teaching of particular sects to the
ground that was common to them all.   The dangers
experienced from the inroads of northern barbarism
on the one hand and of Eastern superstition on the
other, tended to bring about a defensive union among
all genuine Hellenes, and this tendency was even felt,
to a certain extent, within the Christian Church.   It
is curious to see what similar language was used on
this subject by Julian, the enthusiastic polytheist, and
Clement, the Christian saint.   Both of them compare
philosophy to the fire brought by Prometheus from
Heaven to enlighten and cheer the nether world.
Again, Clement says, "Since, therefore, Truth is
one . . . just as the Bacchantes tore asunder the
limbs of Pentheus, so the sects, both of barbarian
and Hellenic philosophy, have done with truth, and
each vaunts as the whole truth the portion which has
fallen to its lot.   But all, in my opinion, are illu-
minated by the dawn of Light."[1]   And Julian : "Let
no man then distinguish or divide philosophy into
many parts, or rather, let no man make manifold that
which is one.   For, as truth is one, so is philosophy
one.   But it is no marvel if we travel to her by
different routes."[2]

The school over which, in the time of Synesius,
Hypatia presided at Alexandria, though owning its
chief allegiance to Plato, borrowed freely from
Aristotle, from the earlier philosophers, from the
Stoics, and from the esoteric doctrines of Greek and
Egyptian priests. Yet its doctrine did not consist of an

" Stromata," c. xiii.   (Wilson's translation.)
Oration against the Cynics.

heterogeneous mass of undigested material gathered
from various sources, but had been reduced to a system
by a master-mind, at once receptive in learning and
original in elaborating—Plotinus, of Lycopolis and
Alexandria. Since the philosophic views of Synesius
were for the most part derived, either directly or indi-
rectly, from this source, it may not be out of place to
give here a slight sketch, not indeed of the whole
system of Plotinus, but of those of his principles
which seem most characteristic of his own mind, or
were most influential among his followers.

The philosophic principles of Plotinus form such
a closely-connected whole that it is difficult to ap-
prehend any of them apart from all the rest, or to
divide his system into the ordinary branches of
theology, cosmology, psychology, and ethics. His
theory of duty and of the virtues depends on his view
as to the origin and nature of the soul, which again is
an essential part of his doctrine of the universe, while
all alike are penetrated and dominated by the thought
of God. If we say that he held the doctrine of the
Trinity, we must bear in mind that some form or
other of that doctrine is to be found among almost
all the thinkers of that age,—pagans, Jews, and
Christians, orthodox or heretical,—that it seemed for
the men of that period a necessary condition of
religious thought. But, though we can find, in the
antecedents and the training of Plotinus, traces of
philosophic Judaism as well as of Christianity,[1] yet

[1] The links are these: Ammonius Saccas, the teacher of
Plotinus, had been brought up as a Christian, and the same
man seems to have been influenced by the philosopher

his particular devolopment of the doctrine is unique, and is necessitated by his own special standpoint. The highest attribute of which he could conceive in the Divine Being was that of unity. Above and beyond all that the mind can ever attempt to reach, he places the One (ΤΟ 'ΕΝ), without qualities, actions, or passions; only to be described by negatives, only to be apprehended in rarely-recurring moments of ecstatic intuition.[1] Yet, though he will not assign any attribute to the One, he seems guilty of a sublime inconsistency in identifying it with the Good. The arguments by which he justifies such a process do not carry much weight, and it seems more reasonable to regard it as a primal act of faith. Next in order to the One, he places Νοῦς,—Mind, or Intelligence,—an emanation and a perfect image of the First Principle, but differing from it in being dual in nature instead of perfectly simple—for all intelligence involves two elements: that which thinks and that which is the object of thought. Within the Divine Intelligence are comprised all the archetypes or the Ideas of Plato, the really existing originals of which all things perceived by the senses are mere phenomenal copies. The creation and ordering of the material universe is not, however, the work of Νοῦς, the functions of which are purely contemplative, but of a third principle, an emanation from Νοῦς, which

Numenius, who was deeply attached to the teaching of Philo. See Vacherot.

[1] The doctrine of the superiority of the One to Intelligence itself, reminds us of the words of St. Paul : 'Η εἰρήνη τοῦ Θεοῦ ἡ ὑπερέχουσα πάντα νοῦν.

resembles it as Νοῦς resembles the One—'Η Ψυχή, the World-Soul, in which all individual souls are comprised, without thereby losing their separate existence. The Soul is the medium between Νοῦς and Matter, as on the one hand it contemplates the ideal archetypes and on the other it produces likenesses of them under conditions of space and time, and thus brings the seminal principles of Being into the regions of Matter, or Non-Being. For Matter is not to be regarded as having a real existence, or even a potentiality of existence, but as an abstraction implied in any negation of intelligible being. It is, in every part of creation, the form, not the matter, that is akin to the intelligible and the Divine. Matter is also to be conceived as the principle of evil, and thus the transitory and subservient character of all that opposes the Divine action affords ground for justifying the providential permission of evil, and for anticipating the final completion and restitution of all things. In this theory of creation, Plotinus was in opposition to two current views : that of the Stoics and other Pantheists, who identified the world, or the World-Soul, with the whole Divine Being ;[1] and that of the Gnostics,[2] who carried their aversion to matter and their sense of general corruption so far as to hold that the whole universe was the work of a fallen and degraded member of the divine hierarchy. The doctrine of Plotinus as to the nature of the human soul is a part of his cosmical theory. Every

---

[1] Plotinus said that God is ἀρχὴ πάντων, οὐ πάντα.

[2] In Synesius, we find several of the names of the Gnostic aeons, Νοῦς, Βυθὸς, Σίγη, and Σοφία.

soul is an emanation of the World-Soul, to which it returns at death. It participates in Νοῦς, and so is able to rise to the contemplation of Divine Ideas. Some of the functions of life belong to the body, others to the soul, others to the intermediate principle of animal life. The great object of life pursued by the will when perfectly free is to rise by the practice of virtue and of contemplation [1] above the world of sense and matter to that of intelligible realities. Neither the understanding nor the ordinary or political virtues are sufficient for this purpose. Above them are the purifying virtues, which discipline the soul till it becomes capable of union with God. Plotinus himself, according to the account given of his life by his disciple Porphyry, endeavoured to bring his practice into accordance with his theory, and succeeded in rising to contempt of bodily cares and needs, and to occasional absorption in ecstatic vision.

It might be expected that so dreamy and mystic a philosophy would rapidly degenerate among the inferior followers of the great master. Porphyry, his most intimate disciple, developed and popularised some parts of his system, and devoted some of his philosophic energy to polemics, in disputes with the Christians. Others, notably Iamblichus, carried further

---

[1] The things that keep back souls from rising to their divine origin are ἡ τόλμα, καὶ ἡ γένεσις, καὶ ἡ πρώτη ἑτερότης, καὶ τὸ βουληθῆναι δὲ ἑαυτῶν εἶναι. There is an interesting correspondence between the religion of Plotinus and the mediæval treatise, "Theologia Germanica," a production of the *Freunde Gottes*.

the theurgic and mysterious part of his doctrine, and
applied the mystic theories of numbers, borrowed
from the revived school of Pythagoras, to the Plotinic
conceptions of the Divine and spiritual nature. They,
consequently, soon became lost in mazy fields, into
which it is impossible to follow them. If we may use
a Coleridgean expression, we would say that, while
Plotinus divided in order to distinguish, they distinguished in order to divide, and to make a separate
entity, or series of entities, wherever they could discern
a difference in function or in manner of presentation.

But from the worst extravagances of Neo-Platonic
mysticism, Synesius was happily preserved. It may be,
that Hypatia, in her studies of the exact sciences, had
acquired a discipline that preserved her and her pupils
from degrading superstitions or vague speculations.
And he was himself gifted with a considerable amount
of practical good sense, as well as with a reverent mind
that could realise the limits of its powers. We have seen
that in his oration before Arcadius, he acknowledged
the purely subjective character of the different attributes which men conceive as belonging to the Divine
Nature.[1] He felt a wholesome desire for reticence in
his attempts to reach towards the Incomprehensible.
Again and again he checks himself when he thinks he
is about to say what had best be left unsaid, and,
above all, he regards as impious and presumptuous
the attempt to represent to the untrained mind of the
unthinking vulgar those doctrines which they are
likely to abuse but cannot understand. In a letter to
his friend Herculianus,[2] he expresses considerable

---

[1] "De Regno," c. v.   [2] Ep. 142.

vexation that parts of the thanksgiving hymn he had
written on his return from Constantinople, which contains expressions of theologic mysticism, have gone
abroad, so that people have been troubling him for
explanations of what he could not or would not put
into popular form. These demands for explanations
would be all the more tiresome from the circumstance
that Synesius was by no means a clear and consistent
thinker. It is impossible to make from his writings a
clear account of his views on the first principles of
things. He never wrote a systematic philosophical
treatise, and his philosophic views are to be gleaned
from his hymns, written rather with a devotional than
with a scientific purpose, and from scattered expressions in his letters, as well as from the digressions in
his various light or serious treatises. We have already
seen that he was never inclined to adhere literally to
the teaching even of those authors whom he most
admired, nor had he the constructive genius to elaborate a new system for himself. Thus, if we regard
his theological views, it is impossible to consolidate
them into a definite creed. Much of what he says
agrees with the doctrine of the Trinity as held by
Plotinus. He addresses the First Principle as the
One and All, the Unity of Unities, the Beginning of
Beginnings. He speaks of the animating Soul of the
Universe as the " Third God,"[1] and of the motions of
the heavens as an imitation of the operations of the
Divine Mind.[2]　But he does not, with Plotinus,

---

[1] "De Insomniis," c. i.

[2] Τὸ μακάριον οὐρανοῦ σῶμα οὗ καὶ τὴν κίνησιν νοῦ μίμησιν
εἶναι.—"De Dono Astrolabii."

assign to the World-Soul the entire work of creating
and animating the visible universe, and leave to Νοῦς
a purely contemplative existence, with the production
of archetypes, but states that Νοῦς itself has descended
to matter, to organise and to preserve it.[1] And in
another poem[2] he seems to conceive of the Spirit
(Πνοιά) as originating the creative Logos, rather than
as directly animating the world. But where he is
inclined to draw a veil of mystery, it would be vain to
attempt to strain his words into a consistent clearness.
In expressions which some commentators have supposed to be directed against the Arians,—though it is
to be feared that they might apply to some, at least,
of the orthodox,—he inveighs against the presumption
of attempting to fathom[3] the mystery of the eternal
generation. Amidst the haze of metaphysical theology, he retained firmly the idea of one Divine Power
manifested in diverse forms, and his religious instinct
prompted him to regard himself as standing in direct
relation to that Power, and to address his thanks-
givings and his petitions to the " One Root and One
Fountain,"[4] rather than to any of the intermediary
beings of the celestial hierarchy.

Synesius believed in occasional supernatural communications between God and the human soul. It
is rather startling to find what is to-day the chief
argument against the miraculous or the magical—
the essential unity of nature and the universal pre-

---

[1] Hymn I., l. 81 et seq.   [2] Hymn IV., l. 95 et seq.
[3] Hymn III., ll. 253, 7.
[4] See Hymn II., of which a free translation is given in the
Appendix.

valence of natural laws—used by Plotinus, and, following him, by Synesius on the opposite side.[1]   For
if the whole system of things is bound together as
one vast organism, there must be such sympathies
existing among the several parts as would enable
us, if we had sufficient knowledge, to discern many
signs of future or distant events in what is close at
hand.   He held in contempt most of the thaumaturgic
arts practised at that time, but attached great importance to dreams.   His theory of the imagination,
based mainly on Plotinic psychology, is interesting
and highly idealistic.[2]   The image-producing faculty
belongs to the borderland between body and soul,
and is closely allied to what is called the psychic
pneuma, or pneumatic psyche, a term loosely translated by the schoolmen's expression of *animal spirits*.
This faculty conveys to the consciousness some and
not others of the phenomena presented to it, according
to the degree of purity to which the soul has attained.
As the images even of sensible things cannot be
apprehended except by means of the image-producing
faculty, it would seem that a moral element is introduced even into the act of perception.   But whether
Synesius intended or not to go as far as this in
subjective idealism, he certainly held that when, as
in dreams, the impressions received do not come.

---

[1]   "De Insomniis," c. i.

[2]   He says, in one passage of "De Insomniis," that as, according to the old philosophy, Νοῦς comprehends in itself the
forms of all that *is*, and Νοῦς is to Ψυχή as that which *is* to
that which *becomes*, so Ψυχή must comprehend the forms of all
that *becomes*, and that has but a temporary and apparent existence.—See the whole of chap. iii. of "De Insomniis."

directly through the senses, it is the pure soul only that can receive by their means communications of truths vouchsafed by heavenly powers. And thus it is within the power of all men, by purifying their souls, to elevate also the imagination, and obtain for it some share in the upper light.

But, in general, he regards the divine operations as carried on by the ordinary laws of nature. His theory of Providence, glanced at in many parts of his writings,[1] is clearly set forth in his treatise of that name. He endeavours to reconcile the idea of the divine government of the world with that of human freedom and responsibility. He makes the father of Osiris warn him not to rely on the active intervention of the gods to counteract any mistake that he may make. Among the gods, he tells him, there are some that enjoy the bliss of always contemplating the divine perfections, others that concern themselves with the things of the world.[2] The divine impulse by which all things are ordered is not communicated directly to the lowest parts of creation, but from the highest order of beings to those next below them, and so on to the bottom of the scale. Thus the powers of the conflicting elements and the inferior dæmons are very far removed from the divine beginning. Yet, to keep the world from perishing utterly, divine power is transmitted even to them ; but it comes fitfully, as the pulls of a cord that moves a puppet-show. The spirits who convey this power do so, not as their noblest function,

---

[1] *e.g.*, in " De Regno," c. xxi.

[2] A distinction corresponding to the Plotinic Νοῦς and Ψυχή.

which is purely contemplative, but as a matter of
necessity, just as the philosopher reluctantly attends
to his every-day business. The eyes by which action
is guided must be shut before the contemplative
eyes can see clearly.[1] The gods are not to be
hastily summoned from their sphere of beatific contemplation. It is for men to try to rise to them.
They prefer to commit their authority to a few good
men, or heroes, who have to take thought for the
many. These men maintain a constant struggle
against the spirits of matter, or dæmons, who assail
them first from within, by stirring strife among their
passions, and then, if unsuccessful, from without,
by inciting evil men to resist their authority. This
struggle is permitted in order that character may
be strengthened. Providence does not treat men
as new-born babes, from whom all dangers have to
be averted, but encourages them to exert their
powers to the utmost.[2] Later on, in the treatise,[3]
he returns to the problem of the co-existence in
the world of good and evil, and, in the spirit of
the earlier Stoics,[4] hints at a solution by showing
how, in every field and garden, the foul is purified
by being made to pass through the roots of what
is wholesome.

---

[1] See the same simile in the "Theologia Germanica."

[2] "De Providentia," Bk. I., cc. ix.-xi. Compare, as to the
battle against evil, "De Insomniis," c. v.

[3] "De Prov.," II., c. vi.

[4] Compare, in the hymn of Cleanthes to Zeus :

Ἀλλὰ σὺ καὶ τὰ περισσὰ ἐπίστασαι ἄρτια θεῖναι,
Καὶ κοσμεῖς τὰ ἄκοσμα, καὶ οὐ φίλα σοὶ φίλα ἐστίν.

In his views as to practical life and morals, Synesius followed Plotinus and the other Neo-Platonists, in placing, as the final goal to be aimed at, a pure, contemplative, and tranquil state of mind, undistracted by fierce passions, gross appetites, or the importunate demands of worldly affairs. We shall see the effects of this theory on his own later life—how, for him, to be compelled to live under circumstances that rendered tranquillity almost impossible involved the loss of all happiness and satisfaction. But though his aims were as high as those of Plotinus, and he expressed his aspirations in almost the same words,[1] his healthy animal tastes led him to adopt rules of life very different from those of his master. While Plotinus could hardly bear to realise that he was subject to the necessary conditions of physical existence, Synesius aimed at keeping a "sound mind in a sound body."[2] We have seen how, in his "Dion," he vindicated his manner of life against those who practised or professed a stern asceticism He justifies the use of pleasure in moderation. Men cannot live as if they were all spirit. God has given pleasure as a girdle to bind the soul for a while to her bodily habitation. Men who take no reasonable recreation are likely to fall into evil habits. Apathy is an attribute of the Divine Nature only. Human beings should cultivate moderation, not insensibility. Even the Egyptian monks take up basket-making as a recreation. But the Greeks are superior to the barbarians, in that their relaxation is

---

[1] Those quoted at the beginning of this chapter.

[2] Ep. 57.

akin to their work, and made auxiliary to it. A few
rare spirits may reach the desired goal by the purely
ascetic route, but for most men it is better to proceed
ladder-wise than by attempts to fly.[1]

While his sound judgment and healthy tastes preserved him from a rude asceticism, his strong sense
of duty, inherited with his Spartan blood, kept him
from another danger frequently attendant on religious
mysticism—the tendency to neglect ordinary morality,
and to regard right conduct as of less importance
than exalted feeling. But Synesius derived his
moral principles more, perhaps, from the Porch than
from the Academy. Stoic doctrines had before his
time found a congenial soil among the law-loving,
proud-spirited Dorian races,[2] which easily recognised
in Duty the voice of a supreme Lawgiver, and readily
adopted the Socratic principle so prominent in the
Stoic creed, that the good man should be independent
of all possible external circumstances. Synesius,
like Marcus Aurelius and other Stoics, liked to compare life to a great drama, in which the stage-manager
assigns the parts to each actor, and each receives
praise or blame, not according to the dignity of the
person he represents, but according to the diligence
and skill of his own representation.[3] It is interesting
to observe the spirit of almost military obedience in
which he received his call to duty on the important
occasion of his election to the bishopric : " I will

[1] "Dion," vi., vii., viii., &c.
[2] In illustration of this point, see Plutarch's "Life of Cleo-
menes."
[3] "De Providentia," I., c. xiii.

bow to necessity, and accept this office as a pledge from God. For I consider that if the command had come from the Emperor, or from some miserable Praefectus Augustalis, and I had disobeyed, I should have been punished. But we should obey God without compulsion." The sentiment is exactly that of the Stoic Cleanthes.[1] And that the Stoic idea of the insignificance of all that does not belong to conduct was maintained by him to the last is shown in a letter[2]—perhaps the last he ever wrote—in which, after relating his bitter trial, he says : "But I still hold the doctrine that the things which happen to us are in themselves neither good nor evil ; or rather, what was formerly learned as a lesson, is now a principle fixed in my soul, thus exercised by calamities."

It is evident, from this sketch of the chief principles recognised by Synesius in thought and in action, that for him, as for all of his school, philosophy and religion were inextricably bound together. It would probably have been impossible for him to conceive that there could ever be any opposition between the two, though it seemed natural enough that there should often be opposition between philosophy and the popular beliefs attendant on every form of religion.

[1] As quoted in the "Enchiridion" of Epictetus. We may compare the thoughts of Julian on his elevation as Caesar : "Wouldst thou not be angry if one of thy beasts, a horse or a sheep or an ox, were to run away and deprive thee of its use ? . . . . and wouldst thou, being a man and no beast, withdraw thyself from the gods, and care not to what purpose they might use thee ? "—Julian, Letter to the Athenians.

[2] Ep. 126.

The early Neo-Platonists used the polytheistic mythology with the greatest freedom, and modified or re-
interpreted the old stories to make them illustrate
various parts of their philosophy. They could receive the gods of popular belief into their system
in three distinct ways. Plotinus applied the myth
of Uranus, Cronus, and Zeus to his doctrine of the
One, Intelligence, and the Soul,—identifying, or at
least comparing, one of the chief deities with each of
his first principles ; or again, all the greater gods might
be considered as existing in Νοῦς,[1] and as having
their being in the regions of pure intelligence. But
most of the familiar creations of Greek mythology
lent themselves more readily to the conception of a
multitude of spirits animating different portions of the
universe while still united in the general soul. Almost
any set of popular beliefs, if freely handled, might by
these philosophers have been used as vehicles of a
higher meaning. Their opposition to Christianity was
perhaps in great measure due to the difficulty of treating any portion of its doctrines with a similar freedom.
Porphyry, as we have seen, wrote against the Christians. Iamblichus developed in opposition to them a
system of polytheistic doctrine and discipline. Julian
devoted his whole mind and all his active energies to
the conflict on behalf of Hellenism, using, meantime,
the old myths with a freedom that might sometimes
seem inconsistent with respect. But, after he had
failed, and the faint flicker of the artificially-revived
system had died away,—when Christians had obtained

---

[1] Synesius, "De Insomniis," c. i.

the control of education, and absence of rivalry was
tending, in some regions at least, to make men more
tolerant,—it became possible for a man to be a
genuine Hellene, and yet not hostile to Christianity,
to recognise many of the principles of the best
philosophers in the doctrines of the Church, or even,
after the temples had been closed, to satisfy his
religious desires by worshipping in Christian churches
and seeking participation in Christian mysteries. This
was what happened in the case of Synesius. He had
been accustomed to use the heathen mythology
wherever it served his purposes ; but the polytheistic
system seems never to have had on him the hold that
it had on Iamblichus or on Julian. In his treatment
of the august person of Osiris, for example, he is very
much more free and anthropomorphic than Plutarch
had been in handling the same subject.[1] He was able
to think of the gods as forms of Νοῦς, or as powerful
angels ; and it seems to have been by a gradual and
not a sudden process that he ceased to regard them
as objects of worship, while he retained his belief in
the angelic hierarchy, and, by the help of the Christian
doctrine of the Logos, came to identify Νοῦς with the
person of Christ. We shall have to study hereafter the
attitude in which he stood towards popular Christianity
at the time when the bishopric of Ptolemais was first
offered to him. Here we would only observe that,
before he definitely threw in his lot with the Christians, his position, though one of complete freedom,
can hardly have seemed quite satisfactory to himself.

---

[1] See his " De Osiride et Iside."

His sensitive nature was stung by reproaches of men who were, he felt, aiming at the same objects as he was. Nor were those reproaches entirely unmerited, for there seems some strangeness in hearing a disciple of Plotinus, an aspirant after the beatific vision, declare that his life consisted in reading and hunting, while occupied in such trivial work as the "Praise of Baldness," and reading chiefly such shallow writers as Dion Chrysostom. He may, perhaps, have felt the sentiment expressed in the lines of Wordsworth :—

> Me this unchartered freedom tires,
> I feel the weight of chance desires,
> My hopes no more would change their name,
> I long for a repose that ever is the same.

Both his religious aspirations and his constant craving for human sympathy would seem to suggest to him that he should openly join himself to those who were professedly endeavouring to purge society of its corruptions, and to raise their own lives nearer to the ideal perfection. And these suggestions were made more powerful by the combination of circumstances which forced him to make a definite choice.

CHAPTER V.

SYNESIUS AS BISHOP-ELECT OF PTOLEMAIS.

Τοῦ Θεοῦ δὲ ἐπενεγκόντος οὐχ ὅπερ ἤτουν ἀλλ᾽ ὅπερ
ἐβούλετο, εὔχομαι τὸν γενόμενον νομέα τοῦ βίου
γενέσθαι καὶ τοῦ νεμηθέντος προστάτην, ὡς μὴ φανῆναί
μοι τὸ πρᾶγμα φιλοσοφίας ἀπόβασιν, ἀλλ᾽ εἰς αὐτὴν
ἐπανάβασιν.[1]

IT is almost always a futile task to attempt to estimate
the relative importance of outward events and of
inward tendencies in determining the course of any
man's life and the development of his character.
Where some sudden change in circumstances seems
to produce an equally sudden change in disposition
and in motives of action, a more complete knowledge
would probably show that mental and moral causes
had long been working unseen, accumulating the fuel
which some spark from without would be certain to
light upon sooner or later, so becoming the occasion
rather than the chief cause of the conflagration.
And, on the other hand, the successive stages reached,
apparently in the natural course of development, by
any individual mind and character are most frequently to be associated with some changes of fortune
which suggest new ideas or awaken slumbering faculties.   In the case of Synesius, it might be rash to

[1] Syn., Ep. 95.

assert that, but for his unexpected and undesired call to a high ecclesiastical dignity, he would have spent the rest of his days as a philosophical free-lance,—sympathising with good men and good work everywhere, but not closely associated with any religious society,—ready to accept suggestions of truth from all quarters, without formulating any definite creed,—forward in helping either individuals or the State in seasons of distress, yet not clothed with any public functions. His reputation for strict sense of duty, for kindness to friends and to inferiors, for brightness and geniality of temperament, might have been expected to force him, sooner or later, out of his retired and independent position. But the call from retirement to publicity came in a form that necessitated, as he himself said, a change in all his habits of life, and this change, apart from the severe trials and temptations to which he was from this time onward continually exposed, could not but have a reflex influence on his tone of mind, which may be traced in the writings, scanty and short though they be, of his later years.

But those who, rightly regarding Synesius as an honest searcher for truth, who was led through Plato to Christ, would seek, at this crisis of his life, for anything adequately corresponding to the term *Conversion*, must be entirely disappointed. We find no trace in his life of that kind of mental conflict described in the "Confessions" of St. Augustine—no agonies of remorse from a newly-awakened conscience; no triumphant exultation over a newly-discovered way of deliverance; no unsparing condemnation of all past life and actions before the date of the new birth. So far is Synesius, when bishop, from regarding his former philosophical life as having been passed "in the gall of bitterness and the bond of iniquity," that he always looks back upon it as a peaceful and blessed time, a season when he could serve God with a quiet mind, as he could never again after he had accepted the distracting cares of office. He did not break with his old friends (though we lose sight of several during his latter years), nor with his old modes of thinking. If there seems to be a breach of continuity in his intellectual and spiritual life, it is not that the man himself is radically changed, but that he has been forced to direct his energy of body and soul along new and less peaceful channels.

The ecclesiastical historians [1] who wrote nearest to the time of Synesius, while proud of his learning and accomplishments, generally represent him as having, up to the time of his election, stood towards the Church in the attitude of a sympathetic outsider, and (as we should naturally suppose from his own writings) as not having yet been baptised. As by the Canons of the Council of Sardica (349 A.D.) no man was to be appointed to a bishopric who had not successfully filled the inferior posts of reader, deacon, and pres-byter,[2] there is something altogether irregular and extraordinary about the appointment, which can only be explained by the peculiar circumstances of the

---

[1] Photius, Evagrius, and Suidas.—See Introduction to the Migne edition of the works of Synesius.

[2] See Bingham's "Christian Antiquities," Bk. II.

time, and the character of the persons upon whom the responsibility of the choice rested.

The chief grounds for the appointment of Synesius are to be found in the miserable state of the Pentapolis at that time, and the probability generally felt, based on the previous services of Synesius and on his influence with powerful people, that he would be able to find a remedy for the prevalent distress. The enemy now devastating those regions was a tribe which Synesius calls the Ausurians and Ammianus Marcellinus the Austurians, and who seem to have been more formidable even than the Macetæ, whose ravages had been felt seven years before.[1] These were, however, for a time kept at bay by a young and skilful general named Anysius, at the head of a very inadequate force of mercenary barbarians.[2] And it was probably just at this time that the able and upright *præses* Gennadius was replaced by the lawless and tyrannical Andronicus, the character of whose administration we shall see shortly.[3] At the same time a change had occurred in the imperial government, which was decidedly for the better. The Emperor Arcadius had died in the early summer of the year 408 A.D., leaving as heir a child eight years

[1] Syn., " Catastasis " i.

[2] Unnigardæ—probably Huns.

[3] Clausen thinks that the letter from Synesius to Troilus, complaining (not by name) of Andronicus (Ep. 73), was written before his ordination; and that as in Catastasis i., which evidently was written after that date, Gennadius is mentioned as *præses*, that Gennadius, or another man of the same name, followed as well as preceded Andronicus ; but the exact chronology of these events is very hard to determine.

old, Theodosius the Younger. During the minority
of the emperor, the government was carried on by
the Prætorian Præfect Anthemius, a man of great
political sagacity, and on terms of intimate friendship
with the members of that learned circle into which
Synesius had been admitted during his embassy in
Constantinople.[1] These men—among whom were the
correspondents of Synesius, Theotimus, Nicander,
and, most influential of all, Troilus the Sophist,—were
continually consulted by the præfect on matters
of state, and there seemed some solid ground for
the hopes of a philosophic monarchy which Synesius
had expressed in his oration "Concerning Kingship," and which sanguine young politicians had
clung to, in spite of continual and bitter disappoint-
ments, from the days of Plato and Dionysius downwards. Synesius himself, though less inclined than
in his younger days to expect great results from
legislative enactments or administrative changes, was
glad to use his influence with the "best of philosophers," as he called Troilus, and the other friends
of Anthemius, on behalf of the suffering Pentapolis.
It was probably this power of influence, as much
as any other qualification, which marked him out
in the eyes of the people as the most suitable candidate for the bishopric of Ptolemais, which seems
to have become vacant in A.D. 409.[2] Those who have

---

[1] Socrates, "Eccl. Hist.," VII., i. ; and Syn., Ep. 49, 47,
26, 73, 75, &c.

[2] The date is elaborately discussed in Clausen (sect. 12), and
is determined chiefly by (1) the interval of seven years which
seems to be implied in Catastasis, i., between the invasion

studied the history of this period, and know what an intense interest was taken by the common people in the current disputes on doctrinal theology, may feel surprised that we hear of no objection made by the people against Synesius on the score of orthodoxy. But it seems probable that this excited and abnormal regard for the most mysterious dogmas of the Church was confined to the populations of large towns like Alexandria, Antioch, or Constantinople, and was even there closely associated with personal esteem or aversion towards those influential men with whom, as champions, the various dogmatic causes were severally identified. The mob of the large towns might not be able to give clear definitions of substance, similitude, or generation, yet might know very clearly whether it preferred Athanasius or Gregory, Meletius or Euzoius, Macedonius or Paul. And in the country districts and the decaying towns of the Pentapolis, which had probably felt but a distant ripple from the storm-wave of controversy in Alexandria, personal considerations were still more likely to prevail over theological. Synesius would, if chosen, be both willing and able to press the cause of his flock among the highest authorities of the State. His character was highly respected.[1] Besides

of the Macetæ and that of the Ausurians; and (2) the reference in Ep. 66, written within a year of his appointment, to the end of the dispute with John Chrysostom, which he places three years from that time. Chrysostom died in 407.

[1] See the testimony, already referred to, of Photius and Evagrius; though Photius commits the blunder of making him bishop of Cyrene.

being an energetic patriot, he was known to be a
man of devout disposition, who made pilgrimages,
was friendly with priests,[1] and wrote religious poems,
which might not be easy to understand, and which
he might not be willing to expound, but which were
undoubtedly the product of a pious and faithfu
mind. In times such as those, when the office of
bishop was certain to prove no sinecure, was it likely
that any more suitable person could be found to
undertake the arduous duties?

Such, probably, were the arguments that had most
weight with the people of Ptolemais, whose voice
must be consulted in the matter, and who must have
regarded Synesius, though not a fellow-citizen, as a
benefactor to the whole Pentapolis. But the assent
of the people, though an indispensable part, was not
the whole of an episcopal election. The first choice
of a metropolitan bishop rested with the other bishops
of the province; but in this case, when the unsettled
state of the country rendered communication difficult,[2]
probably not many of the clergy could be assembled
together, and among those who met for the purpose
of election, Synesius was likely to be popular, as
certain to prove an easy superior under whom to
work, and a bold champion of their rights if attacked
by the secular power. But there was another person
whose approval was necessary to confirm the election
—that of the patriarch of Alexandria. That office was
still held by Theophilus, whom we have already seen
exercising to the utmost the ecclesiastical authority

---

[1] I gather this from Ep. 54.   [2] Ep. 13.

which had now for many years been in his hands,
and an inquiry into whose character seems necessary
to explain the course of events at this singular
juncture.

The chief doings of Theophilus, as related by the
usually sober and moderate Church historian, Socrates, gives us the impression of a character almost
unrivalled in ecclesiastical annals for violence, du-
plicity, cunning, and malice. It might be suspected
that the historian was prejudiced by his admiration
for the worthy man whom Theophilus hunted to
death—John Chrysostom, of Constantinople. But
Socrates is no hero-worshipper, and is quite ready
to acknowledge some faults in John, especially his
unnecessary harshness and want of moderation, and
his susceptibility to the influence of a friend, the
presbyter Serapion, less moderate than himself. And
if we had no information about Theophilus beyond
what can be gathered from his own correspondence
with Jerome and the letters of Synesius concerning
his election, the opinion we should arrive at would
not be different from that of the reader of Socrates,
—or rather the testimony of the historian is needed
to clear up difficulties raised by the perusal of the
two sets of letters. For the letters of Theophilus
published in the works of Jerome (who translated
them into Latin, with many apologies for the de-
ficiencies of his rendering) are, for the most part,
written to confute and denounce the opinions of
Origen, on grounds which would have made it impossible, if he had been an honest man, to ordain,
with open eyes, a man holding the views of Synesius.

For if the highly-spiritual optimism of Origen caused his condemnation as a heretic, the vague Platonic mysticism of Synesius might stigmatise him as no better than a pagan. But if, to explain the anomaly, we refer to the history of Socrates,[1] we find that Theophilus was not in earnest in his efforts against Origen, but merely trumped up the accusations against his doctrines to satisfy a private grudge,— first against some learned and pious Egyptian ascetics, and then against John Chrysostom. Socrates relates how Theophilus, who was undoubtedly a cultivated man,[2] was fond of the writings of the philosophic apologist, and consequently became obnoxious to a large party among the Egyptian monks, who seem, with a few exceptions, to have been a very ignorant and illiterate set of men. He escaped their censure by the use of ambiguous language, and by asserting his agreement with them and his dissent from Origen. Meantime he attracted into the service of the Church four ascetics, brothers, called, from their stature, the "Long Monks," who were very much superior in learning to most of their brethren, and whose strict integrity made it impossible for them to continue long to work harmoniously with a man like Theophilus, who is asserted by an independent authority[3] to have had a propensity to accumulate gold and precious stones. Turning against them, Theophilus avenged himself on their criticism by stirring up against them the whole rabble of ignorant monks, accusing them of not holding the doctrine,—which sounds absurd

---

[1] Book VI.   [2] See Jerome's Letters, especially 99.
[3] A letter of Isidore, bishop of Pelusium.

and blasphemous to modern ears,—that the Deity
has a human form, with all the bodily organs of a man.
The strife thus aroused between the Origenists and
the Anthropomorphitæ, as the two factions were called,
was so hot that the "Long Monks" had to flee for their
lives. They took refuge in Constantinople, hoping
to find a redresser of their wrongs in the bishop,
John Chrysostom.   Now, Theophilus had been
opposed to the appointment of Chrysostom, desiring
the see of Constantinople for one of his own presbyters, and had long been eagerly watching for some
handle to use against him.   Besides some other
charges, into which we need not here enter, Theophilus now used against John Chrysostom the accusation of favouring the Origenists, and, with a refine-
ment of malice, used as his instrument a good,
simple-minded man who was not naturally addicted
to controversy, Epiphanius, bishop of Cyprus.[1] This
man was induced by Theophilus to go to Constantinople, to refuse all friendly overtures from Chrysostom, to trespass upon his jurisdiction, and to
insist on the condemnation of the Origenists, and the
accusation of the bishop as their abettor. Chrysostom
was too busy with his own efforts in denouncing vice
in high places and endeavouring to bring about a
reform in morals to occupy himself in judging and
condemning good men of past times. He tolerated
the conduct of Epiphanius till it became quite un-
bearable, and then sent him a message denouncing,

---

[1] The authority chiefly followed as to this controversy is
Socrates. Other records represent the normal character of
Epiphanius in a different light.

in a few terse sentences, his illegal and mischievous proceedings, and warning him of the danger he was thereby likely to bring upon himself. The poor old bishop seems to have been so frightened at the threat, that he took ship at once, and,—overcome, perhaps, by the cares of his late uncongenial occupation,—died before he could arrive at home. But the purpose of Theophilus was delayed, not frustrated, by this temporary failure. Soon afterwards, John, like his adversary, Eutropius, had to experience the wrath of the Empress Eudoxia. He had preached a sermon against the weaknesses of the female sex, which the people of Constantinople, unwilling to apply it to themselves or to their wives, had considered as specially directed against the empress, while she justified its application to her own character by treating it as a personal insult. Now, under the imperial shelter, all the enemies of Chrysostom, from whatever causes, Theophilus being foremost amongst them, swooped down upon their prey. A synod was held at a place called "The Oak," in the suburbs of Chalcedon. Chrysostom was summoned, and, when he declined to appear, was sentenced as contumacious, and deposed from his see. He complied, and went into exile. But the voice of the people, not often, at that time, loud and influential in a good cause, insisted on his return, and Theophilus, with his partisans, was obliged to beat a speedy and ignominious retreat. The resentment of the empress, however, remained unappeased. Chrysostom soon incensed her yet further by opposing the adulatory homage paid to her statue. Another synod was summoned against

him. We do not hear that Theophilus attended it--
his previous experience was not so pleasant as to
make him desire its repetition; but the bishops
present were, no doubt, acting under his influence.
Chrysostom was accused of having returned without
legal authority, and was again banished. Accordingly he departed, and soon afterwards died in exile.
But the general opinion as to the justice of his cause
and the wickedness of his accusers was shown thirty-
five years later, when, amid the applause of the
populace, his bones were brought from his place of
banishment to rest in the city where he had achieved
such a well-deserved and unsought popularity. But,
after his personal objects had been attained, Theophilus had no desire to root out from the memory
of men the opinions on behalf of which he had
persecuted to death the saintliest and most eloquent
of his contemporaries. On the contrary, he was
himself fond of reading the works of Origen, and, on
being reproached for this practice, gave the thoroughly
eclectic answer : "Origen's books are like a meadow
enamelled with flowers of every kind. If, therefore,
I chance to find a beautiful one among them, I cull
it ; but whatever appears to me to be thorny I pass
by as that which would prick."[1] To which Socrates
makes the apposite answer that, since the words of
the wise are as goads, those who feel pricked by them
ought not to kick against them.

Such was the man whose influence was one of the
chief factors in determining the elevation of Synesius

---

[1] Soc., VI., xvii. (Bohn's edition).

to the episcopate. It is far less difficult, in the light of these events, to see why he should be willing to ordain Synesius than it is to understand how Synesius came to regard him with any kind of respect. Dr. Clausen[1] has an ingenious theory that their acquaintance began in the high and neutral ground of astronomy—for Theophilus was interested in that science in its bearings on the Easter controversy,[2] and was likely to consult the young mathematician who had constructed the planisphere. Probably, as the intellect of Theophilus was by no means so corrupt as his heart, Synesius at first saw the patriarch only on his best side, and, after he had acknowledged him as his superior, his Spartan loyalty may have checked any inclination to murmur against those in authority. However that may have been, it is quite possible that Theophilus may have felt a desire to secure the talents and energy of Synesius, as he had secured those of the " Long Monks." His avaricious disposition may have prompted him to prefer an honest man who, if not a good manager, was not likely to intercept any of the dues which ought to be sent from the Pentapolis for distribution among the poor of Alexandria.[3] And the pleasure which he secretly took in the writings of men whose heterodoxy he affected to abhor would dispose him to receive favourably the demands of Synesius for the reservation of private judgment on matters of faith.

The way in which the whole affair presented itself to the mind of Synesius, the many conflicting con-

[1] " De Synesio," sect. 16.   [2] Ep. of St. Jerome, 99.
[3] Ep. 67, and notes of Dion. Petavius.

siderations which alternately swayed him, and the conditions under which he consented to accept the office,
are fully set forth in a letter[1] addressed to his brother,
but also designed for the instruction of Theophilus
and his circle of friends and admirers in Alexandria.[2]
This letter is written with all the familiarity and
apparent openness of brotherly intercourse, and at
the same time with the elaborate care necessary in a
document which was of a semi-public character, and
on which a momentous decision depended. It is
throughout so consistent with the character and views
of the man, as expressed in his general writings, that it
is difficult to conceive how some scholars[3] can have
regarded it as an elaborate piece of dissimulation.

He begins by expressing his gratitude to the people
of Ptolemais for having desired to confer upon him
so high an honour,—one little short of divine,—of
which he feels himself utterly unworthy. It is no
new fear with him lest he should sin against God in
seeking honour from men.[4]   He dreads the distractions of public life, as tending to quench the divine
spark within.   Hitherto, his time has been divided
between light and serious occupations.   In his recreative moments he has been free and genial, ready
to associate and make merry with all.   But in his

---

[1] Ep. 105.

[2] Τοὺς σχολαστικούς, variously interpreted as referring to
members of the Museum or to a body of scholars attached to
the household of the patriarch.

[3] Baronius, Taylor, and others.   See Clausen, sect. 19.

[4] This is, as far as I can find, the first attempt at a Scriptural
quotation in the writings of Synesius, and, as might be expected,
it is too inaccurate to be identified.

deeper studies and serious thoughts he has shunned
publicity, and ever kept apart his inmost feelings and
aspirations, as something too sacred for the popular
gaze, as pertaining only to God and his own soul.
But if he accept this office he must at once drop all
his recreative practices, for they are not becoming
in one who has taken upon himself the sacred functions of a priest, and in his religious life and devotional acts he will have no privacy,—for ten thousand
eyes will always be on the look-out for some slip ; he
will have to exchange the freedom of a learner for the
responsibility of a teacher, and to follow customary
rules.   Some great souls may be able to engage in
active affairs and yet to keep the mind always calm
and unpolluted by worldliness.   But he feels that
such a power of abstraction and of throwing off evil
impressions does not belong to his nature.   A further
objection to the acceptance of office is that he is a
married man.   And he is determined not to give up
the wife whom God has given him, or to dissolve the
union which has been consecrated by the hand of
Theophilus himself.   Nor will he adopt the base
course of degrading her from the status of an honourable wife, while continuing to associate with her in an
underhand manner.   But he will retain her as before,
and his desire and prayer is that she may yet bear to
him many dear children.   But these objections are
unimportant in comparison with those he must next
bring forward.   He is a philosopher, and cannot
undertake to root out philosophic principles from his
mind.   Yet between the doctrines held by thinkers
and any which can be received by the ignorant mul-

titude, there can never be a consistent agreement. For the untrained mind cannot endure the full blaze of truth any more than the eye can behold the mid-day sun. There are three generally held doctrines which he can never accept:—That the soul was created after the body; that the whole world will one day be utterly destroyed; and that the dead will rise again in the way commonly supposed,—for he can only accept the doctrine of the Resurrection in a mysterious and figurative sense. To his own higher view of truth he protests, before God and man, he must always adhere; but he will undertake not to attack the opinions of the common people, which are, after all, the highest to which many can attain. But he cannot dissemble his views before those from whom he is to receive his authority, and thus with a lie in his heart enter into the service of the God of truth. It will be hard for him, if he is appointed, to give up his scholarly leisure and his healthy amuse-ments,—to see his beloved dogs pining for the chase, and his bow hanging worm-eaten on the wall. To such sacrifices, however, with the divine help, he may prove equal;—to that of his philosophical opinions— never. But if, now that he has stated all objections, he is still judged worthy of the office, he will under-take it as a heaven-sent task.

This letter is almost as remarkable for what it does not as for what it does say respecting the disqualifi-cations of Synesius for the episcopal office. Thus, he argues the whole question as one of expediency, and passes over the want of legal and canonical right. The canons must have fallen into desuetude in the

turbulence of the times. Still, one might have expected that he would mention them, though it is not
impossible that, having hitherto lived outside the
pale of the Church, he may have ignored the legal
objections to his candidature. If we take up in
order the chief points in his letter, we are first struck
by the high importance he attaches to the priestly
office. It has been conjectured that he may have
read John Chrysostom's treatise "On the Priesthood,"
but it is perhaps more probable that he derived his
views as to the qualifications requisite in a priest from
the writings of the Neo-Platonists, who, since their
philosophy had assumed a definitely religious character, had attached great importance to the way in
which devotional ceremonies were performed, and
the manner of life of those upon whom they devolved.
As, from many passages of his later letters, it is
evident that Synesius regarded as the chief function
of the priest that of praying for the people, rather
than that of instructing them or of working for their
welfare, it is easy to understand the paramount importance he attached to a calm and undistracted
mind, without which no man could be worthy of the
sacerdotal office. It would therefore be grossly unfair
to argue from his expressions as to his unworthiness
that he had hitherto been living an immoral or even
a slightly incorrect life. The faults of which he
accuses himself seem to be only such as are quite
evident to every reader of his letters—a certain
petulance and irritability consequent on a vivacious
temperament, not inconsistent with a generous disposition and a well-directed life, yet needing continual

efforts of self-discipline to avoid sinking into a state of captious fretfulness and habitual discontent.

The objection grounded on his marriage might have been set aside by Theophilus, even if he had been more anxious than he was on this occasion to avoid canonical irregularity. No universal and binding law of the Church had yet been passed to enjoin strict celibacy among the clergy. From early times, the spirit of asceticism had induced many who aspired towards holiness to eschew the married state, and it was considered wrong for a priest to contract a second marriage, which was regarded, by many of the early Christians, as a kind of bigamy.[1] A proposal had been made at the Council of Nicæa to make a fixed rule on the subject of the marriage of the clergy, but it was foiled by the sensible remarks of a tolerant, though celibate, bishop, Paphnutius of the Thebaid.[2] Since that time, however, several councils held in the West had insisted on celibacy as a condition of admission even to the inferior orders of the clergy, but their rule had not been followed in the East.[3] It is probable that Synesius regarded the matter as well from a patriotic as from a religious point of view, and that at a time when the empire was perishing from ὀλιγανθρωπία, it seemed to him more worthy of a good citizen to pray for more children than to encourage men in shrinking from the cares of married life.

---

[1] See Gieseler's "Ecclesiastical History," Period I., sections 53, 73.

[2] Soc., I., xi.

[3] See Gieseler, "Eccl. Hist.," Period II., section 97.

But the most important as well as the most difficult part of this letter is that which deals with the objections on the score of doctrine. The questions arise, Why did Synesius select these three doctrines as those on which he must reserve his own opinions? Were there no other points on which he could not accept the belief of the Church? And in the case of the first doctrine mentioned, was it at that time considered as an essential doctrine of the Church that the body was created before the soul? To explain these difficulties, we must remember that when Synesius wrote this letter he was but imperfectly instructed in ecclesiastical doctrine, and not well read in the Scriptures.[1] And we may partially adopt Clausen's view, that the doctrine of the Resurrection was mentioned as being only one out of several of which Synesius intended to reserve for himself a private interpretation.

But the most important point to bear in mind, in considering the difficulties which the Greek philosophers found in the system of Christian doctrine, is that such difficulties were generally based on a feeling of incongruity of tone, rather than on a want of evidence as to the facts they were required to believe. The objections of philosophers like Celsus and Julian touch, it is true, on points of historical criticism, but their chief weight is always on the metaphysical or the moral side of questions. To men trained in the Alexandrian school, spiritual sympathy or antipathy would be a far more important factor in

---

[1] See Ep. 13.

persuading them to adopt or to reject a religious
creed than any critical examination of its separate
articles.   And if the cause of the hostility and rivalry
which prevailed between Christianity and Platonism
could once be removed, the two systems had so much
common ground, and appealed in many cases to such
similar feelings, that a sympathetic nature might
easily express the teachings of the one in the phrase-
ology of the other, and, with a few exceptions, might
give an assent to the terms in which either drew up its
fundamental beliefs.   This applies most particularly to
that form of Neo-Platonism which Synesius had learned
from Hypatia, and subsequently developed in his
years of studious and devout retirement, and to that
form of Christianity which prevailed among the liberal
and cultivated men who had imbibed the spirit of
Clement and of Origen.   Synesius might make a few
exceptions.   He might hesitate to receive the doctrine
of the physical resurrection of Christ, not because he
regarded it as unsupported by sufficient evidence, but
because it must have seemed to him so intrinsically
improbable that a pure soul, having once disposed of
its " bag of flesh,"[1] should ever voluntarily reassume
it.   But a study of his hymns, and a comparison of
those—in all probability the earlier—which con-
tain only philosophical terms with those in which
he uses Christian expressions, and even addresses
himself directly to Christ, show how easy was the
transference from a semi-Christian Platonism to a
Neo-Platonic Christianity.

---

[1] Φυλακίον τῶν κρεϋλλίων.—Ep. 130.

The doctrine of the Incarnation was readily assimi-
lated to the Alexandrian belief that Νοῦς,[1] the second
person of the Plotinic Trinity, had descended to the
world of matter to organise it, and to bring it into
some connexion with the divine harmony. Again,
we find in Synesius, in spite of a theoretical belief
that all evil is connected with the material and
perishable,—has, in fact, no real existence,—a very
practical realisation, which is as clear in his early as
in his later writings, of the seriousness of the conflict
ever going on between good and evil, and of the dependence of the soul on divine help to prevent it
from sinking in the struggle. His constant and ever-
recurring prayer is for illumination, for freedom from
worldly corruption, for a fuller vision of the divine
glory. And when he has adopted Christian phrase-
ology,[2] he turns to Christ as to the bringer of light to
the world, and prays again and again for a purified
soul that may celebrate aright the divine majesty.
And, while we see throughout his early writings a
mind to which the principal doctrines of Christianity
must forcibly appeal, I fail to discover anywhere a
trace of hostility to Christians as such. In " Dion,"
indeed, he shows his aversion to the life of the monks ;
but there does not seem sufficient basis for those
scholars who have thought his languge to be directed

---

[1] Plotinus did not believe that Νοῦς had so descended ; but
his followers did not agree on this point, and the belief is
certainly found in Synesius. It is remarkable that the very
word used by the Christians (συγκατάβασις) to denote the
Incarnation is used by Julian in a philosophic sense.

[2] See Hymn X., translated in the Appendix.

against Christians in general.[1] Perhaps the respect
in which he differed most from the better educated
among the Christians of Alexandria, and the point
which induced him to vindicate his intellectual liberty
before accepting office, was his aversion to common
theological modes of argument, and constant appeals
to authority, whether of the Scriptures or of the recognised theologians of the Church. We have already
seen his own loose and irregular way of citing authorities, and his dislike of bringing quasi-judicial proceedings into the regions of philosophical argument.
All quotations which he introduces are brought in for
the purpose of illustration—never for that of proof.

The words in which he explains his future principles of private thought and public teaching (τὰ
μὲν οἴκοι φιλοσοφῶν, τὰ δ' ἔξω φιλομυθῶν) are remarkable and easy of misinterpretation. Gibbon, who
is very well disposed towards Synesius, though quite
incapable of appreciating his character,[3] seems to
regard him as standing in a like position with the
sceptical ecclesiastics of the last century, such as
Talleyrand and Sièyes, men with whom Synesius
would have had very little sympathy. But if we
would understand what Synesius meant by the word
φιλομυθῶν we should observe how he uses this or

---

[1] This is the view of Dr. Volkmann. His allusion to attacks
from the "white coats and the grey," in Ep. 153, is understood
by Neander to apply to heathen philosophers and to Christian
monks. But I cannot find any clear statement that the philosophers used to wear white robes.

[2] "Dion," c. 14.

[3] See "Decline and Fall," c. xx., note 118, for a very coarse
epitome of Ep. 105.

a similar expression (φιλομύθος) on other occasions. The word occurs in his description of the childhood of Osiris,[1] and again in his vindication of literary pursuits,[2] and in both places he is insisting on the value of "truth embodied in a tale" as fitting children or unthinking people for the more laborious efforts after a higher knowledge, to which their faculties are not yet equal. We see in his earlier writings how he followed the taste of his school in continually bringing in the old mythological stories to illustrate a higher meaning. Especially that of the Labours of Heracles seems to symbolise to him the struggle of the soul with the powers of evil in its efforts towards a purer life.[3] And when we come to observe his method of handling Christian story, we see the same symbolical way of treatment. The feast of Christmas makes him think of the glorious birth-pangs of the expectant soul.[4] In a hymn which seems to have been written for the feast of the Epiphany,[5] he attaches, as many other Christian poets before and after him, a mystic meaning to each of the three gifts of the Magi, as betokening kingship, godhead, and death.[6] Another

---

[1] "De Providentia," I., c. ii.   [2] "Dion," c. iv.
[3] "De Insomniis," c. v.
[4] Hymn V., ll. 56, 57 (unless he is there speaking of the world-soul).   [5] Hymn VII.
[6] The hymn in which this idea is most fully worked out, and which is well known to English readers in the version "Earth has many a noble city," is ascribed to a Spanish bishop, Prudentius, who died about five years before Synesius was made a bishop. Either the symbolism occurred to each man separately, or they derived it from a common source.

hymn,[1] full of curious allusions to pagan mythology
and cosmology, celebrates the descent of Christ into
the world of the dead, causing alarm to old Hades
and to the dog Cerberus; and His return to the
upper air, the region of silence and of glory, whence
He dispenses gifts to gods and men.

But, whatever view the modern mind may take of
the explanatory letter of Synesius, the effect which it
had on Theophilus seems to have been to induce
him to allow to Synesius eight months for delibera-
tion. This, again, was contrary to canon law, which
forbade the duration of an episcopal vacancy for
longer than three months.[2] Meantime, pressure was
put upon Synesius to induce him to overcome his
scruples. The chief influence which swayed him
seems to have been that of some good old men who
persuaded him that his philosophy would be a help
rather than a hindrance to him, and asserted that
the Holy Spirit is a spirit of cheerfulness, thereby, it
would seem, implying that Synesius had an over-
strained notion of the preternatural gravity required
in a priest, and that it might not be inconsistent
with the episcopal character to keep dogs and occasionally go a-hunting. Near the end of the time, he
wrote a letter to his friend Olympius,[3] in which he
says that he would far rather die than accept the
office; but that, if he undertakes it, it shall not be for
him an abandonment of philosophy, but a renewal

---

[1] Hymn IX.

[2] Or, rather, probably, to the customary practice, afterwards
framed into a canon by the Council of Chalcedon.

[3] Ep. 95.

of philosophic effort. If he finds the life of a bishop incompatible with that of a philosopher, he thinks of sailing away to Greece, for he cannot endure the reproaches of his fellow-countrymen. At the same time, he wrote to the clergy of Pentapolis, expressing similar hopes in very similar words.[1] He assures them that, in the matter of this election, it is not they that have overcome him, nor has he overcome them, but it is the work of God, who has appointed for him another life than that which he had desired. He feels that he is giving up all that, for a man of his stamp, can make life worth living, and asks for their prayers and for those of all the people, that what seems impossible may be made possible in his case, and that he may continue and grow in philosophy even after this momentous change.

Such were the feelings of Synesius as he presented himself, first for baptism, then—without passing through the intermediate ecclesiastical grades—for episcopal consecration. Though some critics may discover a touch of vanity in his sensitiveness to the opinion of his countrymen, and of ostentation in the manner in which he counted up the sacrifices he was about to make ; and others may think, as did he himself[2] sometimes in the darker days that ensued, that it was an act of presumption for such an outsider to approach the altar of the Lord ; yet it would be hard to refuse our sympathetic admiration to a man who, reserving only his fidelity to his inmost convictions and to his marriage vow, was

----

[1] Ep. 11.   [2] Ep. 67, end.

content to give up all else that he prized,—learned leisure, cheerful amusements, all freedom,—not of thought, yet of action and utterance,—a willing sacrifice in what he believed, whether rightly or erroneously, to be the cause of God and of the suffering people of the Pentapolis.

CHAPTER VI.

SYNESIUS AS WORKING BISHOP.

Οὕτως ἡμῖν Θεὸς καὶ τύχη περιτίθησιν ὥσπερ προσωπεῖα τοὺς βίους, ἐν τῷ μεγάλῳ τοῦ κόσμου δράματι, καὶ οὐδέν τι μᾶλλον ἕτερος ἑτέρου βίος βελτίων ἢ χείρων, χρῆται δὲ ὡς ἕκαστος δύναται.[1]

WITH the elevation to the episcopate the life of Synesius enters on a totally new phase. It is true that, for anything we can observe to the contrary, his character and tastes are not fundamentally changed, although the development of a mind and character without sufficient chronological data to mark each successive stage of progress is an extremely difficult study. We are exposed to a singular temptation to reason in a circle,—to assign certain letters and other documents to a particular period because of their general tone, and then to argue back from the order thus obtained both to the external events of the different periods and to particular details of mental or moral transformation. But although, in spite of the labour expended on the chronological order of the letters of Synesius, it is not always possible to assign them to the earlier or to the later part of his

---

[1] Synesius, "De Providentia," c. xiii.

I

life, yet those of which the dates are certain are
enough to show that his chief characteristics were
the same all through his life,—that he always retained
his eager, generous, petulant nature, his love of
estimation which more than bordered on vanity,
his impatience under real or supposed neglect, his
warm, self-sacrificing patriotism, his readiness to help
all in trouble, his utter contempt for ignorance and
vulgarity, his proneness to exaggeration, which made
him such a racy story-teller.   But we see the sad
change which has been worked in his life and his
temperament, not only by the harassing cares of an
uncongenial occupation, but by others not connected
with his new office—troubles that came to him not
as bishop, but as citizen and as father.   His love of
letters survives in a yearning after his lost leisure—
his domestic affection in his bitter lamentations over
his successive bereavements.   All literary labour is
at an end for him.   He may cling to the name of
philosopher, he cannot retain that of man of letters.
Worst of all, his personal religious faith is subjected
to a terribly severe strain, while his new conditions of
life render it impossible for him to have recourse to
means which, in times of privacy and leisure, might
have soothed his anguish and renewed his fortitude.
Yet, even to the end, one brighter feature lightens
up the gloomy picture: the man's brave resolution
to do his duty in his own sphere of action,—all
the braver because it was generally unsupported
by success, or even by hope of success, that it was
maintained amid storms of trouble without and deep
.darkness within.

Long before the time when Synesius accepted the
episcopal office, the Church had passed through its
earliest stage of comparatively simple organisation,
and it was still undergoing the differentiation of
functions which belongs to a state of advancing
complexity. Not only had distinctions been made
within the body of the laity professing Christianity,—
a separation into various classes of catechumens,
besides the energumens, the penitents, and the
faithful,—not only had the clergy been separated from
the laity and divided into grades, with bishops, presbyters, and deacons, and intermediate officers and
servants constantly springing up between the ranks,—
but within the highest grade, that of the bishops,
originally supposed to be equal, had arisen a variety
in dignity and authority.[1] It was naturally to be
expected that from early times the position of a
bishop whose see only embraced a few country
villages should be a less important person than the
bishop of a town. As the custom arose of holding
synods of the bishops of a province or similar area,
the bishop of the town where such synods were held
acquired some measure of authority over his brethren.
Again, in the days of the conflict with Arianism,
larger meetings of bishops were convened, and were
presided over by the bishops of the great towns ; and
as, in the East especially, the ecclesiastical arrangements were early accommodated to those of the State,

---

[1] For an account of the various grades of the hierarchy, see,
besides numerous other authorities, Bingham's " Origines
Ecclesiæ," Bk. II. ; Gieseler's " Ecclesiastical History,"
Period I., sect. 68, and Period II., sects. 91, 93.

the bishop of each of the head towns of the dioceses which had been formed for civil purposes by Diocletian and Constantine obtained a position of superior authority and responsibility, which was recognised by the Council of Constantinople (381 A.D.), as the Council of Antioch (341 A.D.) had previously recognised the authority of metropolitans. But even these bishops of superior rank did not all obtain an equal dignity. By the Council of Antioch, the bishop of Constantinople was to rank next after the bishop of Rome. But the rivalry of the great Oriental sees, often stimulated by the theological controversies, which, in return, it contributed to embitter, prevented the growth of a great consolidated Eastern Papacy, having its seat in the centre of the civil government, and exercising an equally wide authority with that of the West. The name applied to the bishop set over the great diocese is generally that of *patriarch*, but this word does not occur till about thirty years after the time of Synesius, who addresses his superior at Alexandria as *archbishop*. The see of Alexandria was always one of the most important in the Church, and the authority exercised thence was established by the Council of Nicæa (A.D. 325). The independence and power of the archbishop of Alexandria were partly owing to the peculiar position of the city and the province, which had also necessitated a special civil organisation, and were partly due to that civil constitution itself. Thus we shall see that the metropolitan bishop of Ptolemais stood in a position of subordination to the archbishop of Alexandria somewhat similar to that of the *præses* of the Pentapolis in relation to the *præfectus Augustalis* of Egypt. An observer who could not see that the future of the world was with the Western races, nor anticipate the coming deluge from Arabia, might have regarded the Pope of Alexandria [1] as likely, in coming times, to be at least as influential an ecclesiastical person as the Pope of Rome.

The see over which Synesius had to preside was not that of Cyrene,—which, though a bishopric, was not a metropolitan see,—but that of Ptolemais, which had lately been made the capital of the province in civil and in ecclesiastical affairs. The acceptance of office on the part of Synesius must thus have involved an immediate change of residence from the city of Cyrene, rich for him in historical associations and in personal recollections, to the comparatively modern town of Ptolemais, which was situated on the coast at some distance to the west of Cyrene, and served as a port for the ancient Barca, with which it is sometimes confounded. His new duties were manifold and complex. It was his business to read the service, to preach, and to administer the sacraments in his own church, helped to some extent by a body of presbyters and deacons. He was also obliged to exercise a general oversight over all the clergy of the Pentapolis, to confirm episcopal elections, to hear complaints, to settle disputes, and to bring important cases under the notice of the archbishop. He had the care of inquiring into the morals of the clergy,

---

[1] The name *Pope* or *Papa* is given by several old authorities to the patriarch of Alexandria.—See Renaudot, "De Patriarcha Alexandrino."

and, to a certain extent, of the laity, and of putting
in force the canons against heretical teachers and
flagrant offenders. Also there must have been a vast
amount of miscellaneous work of the nature of arbitration, mediation, and use of influence in high quarters expected from him by the people who had appointed him chiefly that they might have a fearless
champion against open enemies and unscrupulous
governors. We will consider here the various duties
which were required in the ordinary routine of his
episcopal life, and the way in which he performed
them, and leave for the next chapter those tasks
necessitated by the exceptional character of the
times.

In the first place, then, it was his duty to officiate
in his own church every Sunday, and perhaps also
on the Sabbath,[1] as well as on those feasts and fasts
the number of which was then rapidly increasing.
Since, at this time, the portion of the service to
which any but baptised people were admitted was
very limited, it is probable that Synesius had not
familiarised himself with the service of the church till
shortly before he was required to officiate. The part
of the service to which the general public was admitted
consisted chiefly of psalm-singing, in which the anti-
phonal or responsive method of chanting had shortly
before been introduced, the reading of the Scriptures,
and perhaps a few short prayers, followed by the
sermon. It is probable that, until he felt quite sure

---

[1] It ought to be unnecessary to remind the intelligent reader
that at this time the term *Sabbath* is never applied to the
Sunday.

of his ground, Synesius did not preach in person, but
availed himself either of the services of some presbyter
(deacons had not, as a rule, permission to preach) or
of the liberty allowed to him to read some homily
composed by a noted preacher, by means of which he
might instruct himself and his congregation at the
same time. But a man of so quick and versatile a
mind as was that of Synesius could not find much
difficulty in acquiring the art of preaching, and we
possess fragments from two of his sermons probably
taken down in shorthand by some of his auditors.[1]
We should probably feel some disappointment in
these fragments, which, in regard to eloquence, energy,
and breadth of view, seem very unworthy of the
author of the oration " Concerning Monarchy," if his
letter to his brother and to Theophilus had not prepared us to find him somewhat tongue-tied before so
novel an audience. It is to be remembered, also,
that the portions remaining to us are very incomplete
and the text very uncertain, so that it would be unfair
to judge from them alone as to the preaching power
of Synesius, though there can be little doubt that, if
he had ever acquired much influence as a preacher,
his pulpit eloquence would have been far more
widely known than was actually the case. But, in
fact, Synesius never had either sufficient sympathy
with the common people or sufficient regard for the
art of the popular orator ever to become a favourite
preacher.

[1] We have repeated mention in Synesius of scribes or short-
hand-writers, to whom he seems to have dictated some of his
letters, and who made copies of every document of importance.

The first of the fragments[1] is from a sermon delivered either on the eve or on the morning of some festival. He says that the occasion demands a discourse, but not a long one. By speech, God is honoured, but by brevity in speech the congregation are spared. He goes on to exhort the people to moderation and sobriety in the celebration of the feast —an injunction which, as we know from abundant contemporary evidence, the prevalent abuse of love-feasts rendered very necessary. He points to the incongruity of worship and intemperance. God is "Wisdom and Reason," and stupefying drink is hostile to the reason. Men should rejoice at such feasts, but they should "rejoice with trembling," and their drink should be the "cup of the Lord," which is "the Word of God," as given in the Old and the New Testaments. Here he shows how he had acquired the tone of the preachers of his day in forced interpretation of Scripture, choosing a text which, in the Septuagint version, is utterly unintelligible,—starting difficulties which a slight knowledge of Hebrew would have avoided altogether, using them to prove that the text cannot bear the meaning most easily assigned to it, and finally importing another meaning which cannot possibly have occurred to the mind of the original writer.

The second fragment[2] is shorter, and is addressed to the neophytes who had just been baptised on

---

[1] "Homilia," I., 295-6.

[2] "Homilia," II., 297-8. The passage printed after this fragment has nothing to do with the matter, and is considered by good authorities as an interpolation.

Easter Eve, whom he warns not to fall from
their state of purity. It is of interest, in showing
the persistence of his old habits of thought in
tracing a relation between the created and the
uncreated light, and also the way in which, in
accordance with his former professions, he attached
a spiritual meaning to the doctrine of the Resurrection.

To proceed with the order of the Church service :[1]
after the sermon, the general public departed, though
catechumens, penitents, and energumens, or persons
supposed to be under diabolic influence, were allowed
to remain while the prayers of the faithful were
offered on behalf of each class in turn. Then all
were dismissed except baptised persons, who pro-
ceeded to the *Missa fidelium*, or Communion service.
This comprised, first, the silent prayers ($\epsilon\dot{v}\chi a\dot{i}\ \delta\iota\dot{a}$
$\sigma\iota\omega\pi\tilde{\eta}c$), with collects, the bidding prayers ($\epsilon\dot{v}\chi a\dot{i}$
$\delta\iota\dot{a}\ \pi\rho\sigma\sigma\phi\sigma\nu\dot{\eta}\sigma\epsilon\omega c$), the offertory, the prayers of consecration, the commemoration of saints, a general
thanksgiving, the hymn Trishagion, a general in-
tercessory prayer for living and dead, the Lord's
Prayer, and, after the proclamation, " Holy things
for the holy," to guard against any intrusion of
strangers, communion in both kinds, of clergy and
then of laity ; finally, the benediction and the dis-
missal. The form followed in the Pentapolis was
that of the church of Alexandria, and there is little
doubt that it corresponds almost exactly with the
ancient Liturgy of St. Mark. This liturgy, the

[1] See Bingham's " Origines Ecclesiæ," Bk. X. ; Palmer's
" Origines Liturgicæ," sect. 1, &c.

language of which is simple and elevated, has been repeatedly published in English.[1] We have touched on this matter of the ordinary services merely in order to assist in realising the daily life of Synesius. We do not find many, if any, references to the Liturgy in his writings, for the analogies to be found in his hymns are probably quite accidental.

Another of the duties of the bishop of Ptolemais was to write occasional letters to the clergy of the Pentapolis, if they were ever summoned together on any occasion when he could not be present. The first of his charges,[3]—written, perhaps, while he had not yet returned from his ordination in Alexandria,[4] —is as strange a production of the kind as was ever written by ecclesiastic. He bids them show hospitality to the messenger who has arrived from Alexandria to announce the date of the next Easter festival. The man deserves kind treatment, since, in order that the old customs of the Church may not be broken, he has travelled to them through a country rendered dangerous by the enemy. He then requests that the people of the city be required to pray for himself,[5] and thus to perceive their folly in having

---

[1] It is published in Latin and Greek in Renaudot's "Liturgiarium Orientalium Collectio," and there is an English translation in Neale's "History of the Holy Eastern Church," in Brett's "Collection of Liturgies," and in the "Early Liturgies" of the Ante-Nicene Library.

[2] Bingham, Bk. X., c. iv.

[3] Ep. 13.   [4] Clausen, "De Syn.," sect. 24.

[5] May not this (since prayers for the bishop form part of the Liturgy) be the official notification to the citizens of his acceptance of office?

chosen a man who requires their prayers more than they need his. He supposes that he ought to write to them on this occasion of their assembly, and if he has nothing to say to them of the kind that they are accustomed to hear, they must excuse him and blame themselves, since they have chosen to promote a man comparatively unacquainted with the Scriptures. But Synesius seems on this occasion to have undervalued his own powers. He soon obtained sufficient acquaintance with the Bible to be able to make quotations from almost every part,—quotations which are often very apt, though sometimes strangely loose and inaccurate.

Another important task of the metropolitan bishops was to prevent the intrusion of heretical teachers into their churches and pulpits, a duty which even extended, in some cases, to the expulsion of such teachers from their provinces. We might expect to find that a duty of this kind would be uncongenial, or even impossible, to an honourable man of questionable orthodoxy. But, fortunately for Synesius, the particular heresies against which he had chiefly to combat were of a kind with which he had no sympathy, and the measures which he took against sectaries reflect no discredit on his name. He was a stranger to the stern and uncompromising monotheism which seems to have furnished the basis of the Arian doctrine, and the particular form in which Arianism invaded the Pentapolis was that of Eunomianism,— a system which must have been at least as revolting to a Neo-Platonist as to the most orthodox of the Nicene fathers. Eunomius and his master Aëtius

of Antioch seem to have acquired a slight knowledge
of Aristotelian philosophy and logic, which they used
to defend and maintain some very sensational theses
of their own.[1] The statement which Eunomius is
said to have made (though possibly exaggerated by
his opponents), that the Deity is as ignorant of His
own nature as is the mind of man, can scarcely have
found favour with a follower of Plotinus, who placed
the supreme felicity of the Divine Mind in the perpetual contemplation of eternal perfection. There
is no need to add to the disgust which such irreve-
rence would arouse in the mind of Synesius the
antagonism which, as a Platonist, he might feel
against the methods of Aristotle; for we have seen
that the Alexandrian school aimed at a reconcilia-
tion between the Platonists and the Peripatetics;
but we may certainly add his Hellenic patriotism
and his loyalty to the established order. From passages already referred in "De Providentia," and from
his letters as bishop, it appears that in his early days
he despised Arianism as a religion of barbarians,
and in his later life opposed it in the cause of peace and
order. The injunction he issued to his clergy against
the Eunomians is strict and remarkably energetic.[2]
He is evidently much incensed against the inter-
lopers, "the newly-arrived apostles of the devil and
of Quintianus" (an Eunomian), and orders that they
be tracked out, exposed, and banished. But, at the

---

[1] See, besides the controversial works of Jerome, Chrysostom,
&c., Socrates, "Eccl. Hist.," Bk. II., c. xxxv.; Bk. IV.,
c. vii.; and Bk. V., c. xxiv.

[2] Ep. 5, with which compare Ep. 45.

same time, he is most careful that the orthodox party shall not use a pretended religious zeal as a cloak for selfish greed. The property of the offenders is to be scrupulously respected, and both plunder and the acceptance of bribes are strictly forbidden under pain of excommunication.

One letter remains—and that a very characteristic one—from Synesius to Theophilus, bearing on the disputes concerning Chrysostom. After the exile of John himself, his followers had been subjected to a merciless persecution, for which their conduct in steadily refusing to recognise his successor afforded some excuse. But after the death of John (in A.D. 407), Theophilus seems to have feared a dangerous schism if the disputes were not quieted, and so consented to a general amnesty. But the bishops of the Johannite faction were not all sufficiently confident in the honour of their opponents to venture to return to their sees. One of them, Alexander, bishop of Basinopolis, in Bithynia, who is mentioned in the lives of Chrysostom as one of his staunch followers, preferred to remain in Ptolemais, apparently in the household of Synesius. The bishop was much divided between his natural inclination to hospitality and his respect for the laws of the Church, and wrote to Theophilus a very diplomatic letter,[1] from which nothing can be gathered as to his opinions on the controverted questions, but which shows his peace-making disposition, not without a touch of vanity. He mentions the previous good

[1] Ep. 66.

conduct of Alexander, excuses his friendship for his old patron, expresses his own feeling that death should put an end to all strife. Then, after mentioning the amnesty and Alexander's refusal to return to his duties, he states the course he has hitherto pursued. He has not admitted him to the Communion, nor recognised him publicly as a bishop, but privately he is treating him in a kindly and hospitable way. But, in spite of his precaution, some people take offence; and whenever, on his way to church, he meets Alexander, he looks another way, and feels himself blush. He dislikes the inconsistency between his public and his private conduct, and wants to know definitely whether or not he is to recognise the man as a bishop. Feeling his own inexperience, he has consulted some older men, but he cannot agree with their opinion that an open slight should be shown to their guest on account of an uncertain suspicion.

Another letter to Theophilus relates to the appointment of a bishop for a little place called Olbia, and illustrates the way in which such proceedings, when orderly, were conducted, while it shows how little real authority belonged at this time to the metropolitans, between the archbishop on the one hand and the clergy of the province and the people of the particular see on the other. The people of Olbia had requested him, on the death of their aged bishop, to come and assist at the election. He came accordingly, and, after congratulating the people on having so many worthy men to choose from, recommended a certain Antonius, as being particularly deserving of the office. The people acceded to his proposal, and sanctioned the nomination of Antonius. Two bishops present, who knew Antonius personally, gave their votes in his favour. Then Synesius—who, though he had never met Antonius, had made inquiries concerning him, and satisfied himself that he was a suitable candidate, and would prove a desirable colleague,—added his vote, and accordingly he writes to the archbishop signifying his wish and that of the people, that he will consent to ordain the man they have chosen. It is noticeable that the concurrence of three bishops of the province, required by the Canons of Nicæa[1] for an episcopal consecration seems here to be required for an election, and that the right of finally ordaining rests with the patriarch, whose power is evidently on the increase.

But far the most interesting of the letters of Synesius to his superior, as throwing most light on the state of the Church at this time and on the multifarious nature of his duties, is one which describes a visitation he made through the neighbouring villages to order matters and settle disputes, —one part of his episcopal functions for which he was not wholly unsuited.[2]

His first task was to superintend the election of a bishop for the villages of Palæbisca and Hydrax, situated at a little distance inland from the coast-town of Erythrum, to the see of which they had previously been joined. Theophilus was accused by

---

[1] Bingham, "Origines Ecclesiæ," Bk. II., c. xi., sect. 4.
[2] Ep. 67.

some of his enemies of trying to increase his influence throughout the diocese by appointing bishops devoted to his interests in small country districts that were only entitled to the ministrations of a parish priest. If such was his purpose on this occasion, it was foiled by the extraordinary popularity and possibly the foul play of Paul, bishop of Erythrum, and the whole storm of opposition was directed against the unfortunate metropolitan who was trying to carry out the orders of his superior. Synesius gives, in the letter just mentioned, a graphic but overdrawn and very humorous picture of the whole transaction. He took the journey, he said, in spite of bodily infirmities and the dangerous state of the country, that he might loyally fulfil the demands of Theophilus. It may be mentioned that neither in the case of his episcopal labours nor previously, in regard to those connected with the embassy to the Court, does he seek to minimise the perils and sufferings that he has had to encounter. But self-depreciation is not a common virtue in Greeks from the days of Odysseus downwards, and the tendency to dwell on personal inconveniences encountered in the course of duty is found in so virtuous a contemporary as John Chrysostom. On arriving at Palæbisca, Synesius assembled the people in the church, produced the letters from Alexandria, and ordered them to proceed to the choice of a bishop. But immediately a most tumultuous scene occurred. The disturbance among the people made it impossible to go on with the business, while some men gained points of vantage and harangued the multitude. Synesius

promptly ordered the ringleaders to be arrested and
turned out of the church, and tried to bring the
people to reason. But his efforts were in vain. He
pointed out to the excited assembly the evils of
insubordination, and mentioned the authority of the
archbishop, whose letters he had just delivered to
them. Thereupon they all cried out that their cause
must be brought before the archbishop himself.
Synesius was at his wits' end. The unruliness of the
men was bad enough, but the appeals made to his
feelings by the women—who held up their babes to
him, and pressed forward with eyes shut that they
might not see the empty episcopal throne,—almost
compelled him to yield; and, for fear lest he should
do so, he broke up the assembly, convening another
to meet in four days' time, and denouncing the
severest penalties of the Church against any who
should before that date show the slightest sign of
insubordination. But when the four days had ex-
pired and the second assembly was called, matters
were no better. Men, women, and children clamoured
for Paul of Erythrum,—him and no other would they
have for their bishop. When the deacons[1] com-
manded silence, the shouting was turned into a
prolonged wail, varied by the groans of the men, the
shrieks of the women, and the screams of the
children. In the midst of this hubbub, a paper was
brought forward, and a demand made that it should
be read aloud. It proved to be a statement of the

[1] Synesius does not here use the word διάκονοι, but
ἱεροκηρύκες; but the functions he describes seem generally to
have belonged to the deacons.

K

whole case drawn up to be submitted to Theophilus.
It asserted that there had never been but one bishop
of Palæbisca, Siderius by name, who had been
appointed because Orion, bishop of Erythrum, was
old and soft-hearted—a total disqualification in the
eyes of men who expected to find in their bishop
an active and powerful supporter in secular affairs.
But even this one appointment had been uncanonical,
for Siderius had not gone to Alexandria for ordination, nor had the requisite three bishops of the
province been present at his election,[1] but he had
owed his installation to a single Cyrenean, named
Philo,—a good man in most respects, but rash and
lawless.   Subsequently, Athanasius had recognised
the merits of Siderius by appointing him to the
metropolitan see of Ptolemais.   In his old age he
had returned to his former see and died there, but
had not had any successor; and, on his decease, the
villages had again belonged to the bishopric of Erythrum.   When the people asserted that this arrange-
ment had been sanctioned by Theophilus himself,
Synesius demanded documents.   None, however, were
forthcoming, yet the fact remained that the people
were all entirely devoted to Paul and determined not
to be put under any other bishop.   Synesius was in
great perplexity, and could not in any way determine
whether it were cunning or force or the grace of God
that had given this young man so extraordinary an
influence over the people that to them life without

---

[1] Or consecration, suggests Dion. Petav.   But see case mentioned above.

him seemed not worth living. He could only put the case before Theophilus, and beg him to treat the people with even more than his accustomed kindness.

During the four days that intervened between the first and the second meeting, a matter was brought before Synesius which must have inclined him to the less favourable opinion as to the character of Paul of Erythrum. A dispute had arisen between him and a neighbouring bishop, Dioscorus of Dardanis, as to the possession of a certain hill, which seems to have formed part of the property attached to the bishopric of Dardanis. It had once been strongly fortified, but the works had been destroyed by an earthquake. The present dangerous state of the country, however, made it desirable that it should be re-fortified, and it was, consequently, of value to the possessor. Dioscorus now accused Paul of preventing the use of the height for military purposes by a false allegation that it had been consecrated to ecclesiastical uses, Synesius, who, we have seen, had formerly experienced the benefit of such strongholds, was angry at the frivolous pretext. If, he said, in times of persecution or of war, men are obliged to meet for worship in hidden places, or in private houses, such a fact does not alter the character of those places. Else would every cleft and mountain be an inviolable church. In this case, he made an inquiry into the facts, but could find no record of formal grants. It appeared that Paul had demanded possession of the place, but that Dioscorus had not given it up, and

had gone away, taking the keys with him. Then
Paul had managed to convey a sacred table and other
furniture[1] to the place, and had consecrated a little
chapel on the crest of the hill. At this time there
had been a gathering of bishops in the neighbourhood, who had come together to settle some civil
affair,[2] and they had expressed abhorrence at the
hypocrisy of Paul, yet felt some scruples against
giving up for military purposes a place that had once
been consecrated. But Synesius was of a different
opinion, and thought this a fitting opportunity for
making a distinction between religion and superstition. "For Christians do not hold that the Divine
Presence must of necessity follow mystic elements
and forms of words, as if drawn by material cords;
though it might be so with the spirit of the world;
but that it accompanies a calm and godlike disposition. For where wrath and headstrong anger and
malicious hatred preside at any action, how can the
Holy Spirit be present? Would it not rather, if
present before, flee on their approach? Wherefore
I regarded the consecration as null and void." When
the business of the episcopal election had brought
the metropolitan into the neighbourhood, the decision
of the matter was referred to him. He held a
meeting of all the neighbouring bishops, and the
affair was decided in favour of Dioscorus. At the
same time, a scurrilous writing, addressed to the
archbishop, was produced, in which Paul had slan-

[1] A κατακίτασμα, or curtain.
[2] Κατά τινα σκέψιν πολιτικήν.

dered his brother-bishop. Paul could not disown
the paper, but suddenly disarmed all opposition by
expressing unbounded remorse. Synesius himself,
considering that to do wrong and to repent afterwards is the next best thing to always doing right,
and that faultlessness is not to be expected in mortal
man, received his professions favourably, though
certainly the way in which he told the story was
hardly calculated to give Theophilus a strong confidence in Paul. Dioscorus also, whose opposition
seems to have been made for the sake of principle,
rather than with a view to his own interests, not only
accepted his apologies, but offered conditions concerning the hill. And when Paul refused the com-
promises proposed, he even gave up the whole place,
—the crest, with the vineyards and olive-yards ad-
joining,—into the hands of his rival. We may pre-
sume that the strengthening and fortification of the
height were secured. Synesius seemed satisfied that
peace had been re-established, and commended
Dioscorus warmly for sacrificing personal ends to the
principles of the Gospel and of brotherly love. He
was to be sent as bearer of this letter to Alexandria,
and Synesius added to his other praises of him that
he was a good friend to the poor of that city, had
looked after the lands set aside for them, and had,
by his watchful care, increased the sums which they
received. The story of the whole transaction receives
an almost comic air from the solemnity with which,
in speaking of the bishops, Synesius always gives
them their complimentary titles, mentioning Paul as

"that very reverend gentleman"[1] when he is describing his meanest and most disgraceful actions.

The case next described and referred to Theophilus is that of two presbyters who had quarrelled. One of them, Lamponianus, had been found guilty of some offence against the other, who was named Jason. But he had confessed his fault, and now requested that the temporary excommunication under which he suffered might be removed. Synesius, however, considered that the authority to absolve, under such circumstances, rested with the see of Alexandria. On his own authority, he had only ventured to order that Lamponianus might be received back into the Church if at the point of death. Jason himself was not to be regarded as free from blame, though his manner of inflicting injuries was by the tongue rather than by the hand.[2]

Synesius goes on to complain of the way in which priests accuse one another, to curry favour with the rulers, by giving them an opportunity for seizing on the property of the accused. He begs that general letters may be sent to stop the practice. So will all parties be benefited, those that do the wrong even more than those who suffer. But he thinks it advisable to refrain from naming individual offenders.

The next complaint is against certain wandering

---

[1] Εὐλαβέστατος.

[2] The next portion of Ep. 67, relating to the pecuniary affairs of Lamponianus, is unintelligible to me, and is acknowledged by Dion. Petav. as a "difficilis et salebrosus locus."

bishops, who had been deprived of their sees in time of trouble, and refused to return when allowed to do so. One of these was Alexander of Basinopolis, respecting whom Synesius had previously sent a letter which had received no answer. Against men of this kind, *vacantivi*,[1] as they were called, canons had been passed at Nicæa and at Antioch, but apparently without effect. The remedy proposed by Synesius is, that they be treated as private persons, and not admitted to any sacerdotal functions or privileges until ambition drives them to their official posts, where they may be of some account.

Finally, he requests the archbishop to pray for him, as he is in great need of divine help, while he scarcely dares to demand for himself the aid he requires. He feels desolate and forsaken, and all things are against him, because of his presumption in accepting an office for which his previous life had not fitted him.

The sentiment expressed in these last words of the letter, though it seems due rather to the petulant impatience of a man disgusted with a hated task than to a settled state of disappointment and despair, is of painfully frequent occurrence in the later letters of Synesius, both to Theophilus and to the clergy. It seems as if he would show them that he and not they had been right,—that he was not fit for his present office, and that the responsibility of his failure lay with them. But if the tiresome routine work of his office demanded such constant exertions, and filled

---

[1] Synesius calls them βασκαντίβοι, apologising, as he well may, for the use of such a barbarous word.

him with such gloomy thoughts, much more was it
so with those harder duties which devolved on him as
champion of his flock against the exceptional evils
which were then so sorely harassing them, under circumstances which it will now be our task to investi-
gate.

CHAPTER VII.

SYNESIUS AS CHAMPION OF THE CHURCH.

Τὸ δὲ τῆς Ἐκκλησίας ἦθος οἷον ὑψῶσαι μὲν ταπεινὸν, ταπεινῶσαι δὲ ὑψηλόν.[1]

THE relations between civil and ecclesiastical authorities were, at the beginning of the fifth century, in as fluctuating and unsettled a state as was the organisation of the Church within itself. The adoption of Christianity by the emperors had recognised a new factor in political life, and a curious spectator might have found it difficult to decide whether the change would tend ultimately to increase or to diminish the imperial authority. On the one hand, if the emperors retained with firmness, and used with moderation, that power which they had wielded as defenders of ecclesiastical unity and order since the Council of Nicæa, they might be able to acquire a moral force which would be a most useful supplement to their material resources. It would seem no hard task for them to keep most of the high ecclesiastical functionaries, if not wholly subservient, yet gratefully loyal to the throne, and to derive additional honour in the eyes of the people by means of the eloquence of popular preachers and the politic measures of am-

---

[1] Synesius to Theophilus, Ep. 89.

bitious prelates. But, on the other hand, there had
been moments in the distractions of controversy when
the exercise of imperial power, on one side or another,
had aroused an opposition, for conscience' sake, among
considerable sections of the community; and, even
after unity had been in some measure restored, cases
had occurred in which an impolitic or unjust action
had brought a strong emperor face to face with a
quiet but relentless opposition from some champion
of the Church, relying on the support of two forces
generally neglected in a despotism—public opinion
and natural justice. It is well known how admittance
into the church at Milan was refused by Ambrose to
Theodosius immediately after the massacre of Thes-
salonica; and other instances might be brought to
show the dread of men in authority lest they should
incur the censures of the Church. It was not merely
to the terrors of the superstitious that the clergy owed
this censorial influence. Part of it was due to the
noble and commanding character of the men who had
been attracted into the Church, as a more congenial
sphere of action than was afforded to them by the
State; and who, chosen by the people and regarded
as the natural champions of the oppressed, could
command attention from the highest officials in the
name of religion and of humanity. And if the emperor of the East felt the necessity of complying with
ecclesiastical rules and of maintaining a harmonious
relation with the leading Eastern bishops, it was none
the less necessary for the provincial governors to retain
a good understanding with the bishops and clergy of
the provinces. Where they failed to do so they laid

themselves open to many dangers,—as was notably
shown in the history of Alexandria shortly after this
time.   There were many points on which bishop and
magistrate might come into collision.   The wide and
general powers of arbitration used by the bishop
might interfere with the governmental administration
of justice.   The right of asylum accorded to the
churches — though it was not allowed to convicted
offenders nor to ordinary public debtors—might pro-
tect those labouring under a doubtful charge from
public justice or private vengeance.   Their rights
over all things concerned with their own churches
might be asserted by the clergy against the claim of
the magistrate to affix his own proclamations to the
church doors.   The power of the bishops to convene
public assemblies—whether of laity or of clergy—
made it possible for them to assume the *rôle* of democratical leaders at a time when democratical
influence was to be found sometimes in the Church
but never in the State.   And the censorship of morals,
with the authority of denouncing ecclesiastical penalties, though not yet so powerful an engine in the
hands of the hierarchy as it afterwards became, was,
even now, able to oppose some barrier to lawlessness
and oppression.   If ever a conflict broke out, the
weapons used were not the same on both sides.   If a
bishop were accused of sedition, he might be sentenced
and banished by the secular authority.   If a governor
offended flagrantly, he might be excommunicated by
the bishop.   But the authority of a council was needed
before a bishop could be formally degraded from his
office; and the intervention of the secular power,

which was not, as yet, usually consequent upon excommunication, was necessary before an evil-doer,
condemned by the Church, could be deprived of his
civil functions.

We have already seen that, at the time of the election of Synesius to the bishopric of Ptolemais, a
governor or *præses* had lately been appointed for the
Pentapolis, against whose acts of cruelty and oppression the people hoped to find a champion in their
new bishop. There can be little doubt that his arrival
had preceded the consecration of Synesius, as in the
first letter of complaint addressed to the influential
sophist Troilus, in Constantinople, the writer does
not mention his public office, but makes a personal
appeal as to a friend and fellow-philosopher. The
chief ground taken up in this first remonstrance[1] is
the illegality of the appointment. While in other
parts of the empire it is forbidden to all natives of
any province to hold rule therein, Libya is given over
to self-interested Libyans. After making strong complaints of the lawlessness and rapacity of the present
governor, Synesius begs that Troilus will use his
influence with the præfect Anthemius on behalf of the
old regulation.

In this letter the name of the offender is not mentioned, but statements are made concerning him in
other letters[2] which enable us to form some conception of his character and of the nature of his career.
Andronicus was a native of the Pentapolitan city of
Berenice. He was of ignoble birth,—it was said that

---

[1] Ep. 73.   [2] Ep. 79, 57, 58, 72, 89.

in his youth he used to catch tunny fish,—and entered early into the party dissensions in his native city, acquiring malevolent feelings towards his fellow-countrymen which he was afterwards able but too effectually to gratify.   The means by which he rose to power are not explained, but, as one of his first acts as governor of the Pentapolis was to endeavour to obtain by threats and extortions an accusation against his upright and able predecessor, Gennadius, it seems not improbable that he had previously supplanted his rival by foul means, so as to acquire the post for himself.   However this may be, on obtaining the governorship, Andronicus used it as a means of enriching himself and his satellites at the expense of the community.   Not only did he increase the regular taxes,[1] the collection of which was entrusted to his rapacious underling Thoas, but he used the vilest means to extort wealth from the citizens under all possible pretexts, and even introduced for that purpose into the law-courts hideous instruments of torture,— presses and screws for fingers, feet, nostrils, ears, and lips,—abominations such as had never been seen in Libya before.   He seemed even to take a pleasure in torturing for torture's sake.   At one time, Synesius wrote, there were two sufferers whom he held in reserve[2] to satisfy his cruel desires when he was at leisure from other acts of oppression.   These men, Maximin and Clinias by name, were threatened with death in obedience to a supposed demand made in a dream to the præfect Anthemius, and reported secretly

---

[1] Tironicum (a military tax) and Aulanæa (Ep. 79).
[2] Ἔφεδροι.

to Thoas when at Constantinople. Anthemius had been suffering from a fever, and Andronicus was quite ready to earn the credit of his recovery by the sacrifice of these two men. From this fact it would seem that Andronicus was weak and superstitious as well as wicked, and we know that Thoas was not the only one of his friends who had an ascendancy over him. A certain Julius, whom Synesius had helped, partly through compassion for his wife and children,[1] to escape in a dangerous prosecution, and who had repaid his kindly offices with bitter calumnies, had at first made some opposition to the governor, but subsequently joined his adherents, probably retaining a hold over him by threats of denunciation. Men like Andronicus and his crew were not likely to show much respect for the rights of the Church. He infringed the privileges of sanctuary, declaring that he would snatch his victims rom the feet of Christ Himself. He affixed his proscriptions to the church doors. When the bishop interceded on behalf of an unfortunate prisoner, whose only fault consisted in having contracted a marriage displeasing to the governor, the sole result of the attempted mediation was, that the prisoner was kept in closer constraint, lest a rescue should be attempted, and there was a terrible suspicion that he was being starved to death. Terror prevailed throughout the province, as in a town taken by storm. The misery caused to Synesius was intense. It was not only that his sensitive and sympathetic nature revolted beyond

---

[1] Ep. 94, 50, 79. With the name of Julius is associated, in Ep. 50, that of our old friend John.

measure at the sight of such horrors.   He was compelled to hear complaints against himself as in part
answerable for them.   Every one believed in his powers
of persuasion,—he had believed in them himself;
he had been chosen bishop mainly with a view to the
influence he might exert on behalf of the people, and
it was quite impossible for him to convince the sufferers that he was as impotent as they, and even more
wretched.   At this crisis a domestic calamity rendered
his misery complete.   He had, as we have seen, three
young sons, who had been, with his studies and his
rural pursuits, the great delight of his life.   Now, one
of them sickened and died,—we do not know which
of the three,—the "dearest," his father said, but
probably whichever was lost would seem the dearest
in the first agony of bereavement.   It seemed to
Synesius that an evil fate was pursuing him,—that he
was being punished for some unknown crime.   In
the days of his private life he might have sought for
calm and resignation in a solitary pilgrimage, such as
he had formerly made in the Libyan desert, or have
crossed the sea in search of distractions and of health ;
but now the cares of office and the troubles of his
fellow-citizens left him no leisure for self-recollection,
no means of seeking encouragement and consolation.
"You know," he wrote to his friend, "that a certain
day was foretold for my death.   It was that on which
I accepted the priesthood."   He was driven to the
brink of suicide, till, as he said, "troubles became
my comforters in trouble," and his flagging energies
were aroused to renewed efforts by renewed acts of
villany on the part of Andronicus.   He had written

in vain to Troilus and to another influential friend—
Anastasius. He had exhausted his own powers of
persuasion, and had threatened the governor with the
censures of the Church. One step could yet be
taken. He called an assemby of the clergy, and drew
up a solemn sentence of excommunication against
Andronicus, Thoas, and all their adherents. At the
same time, he addressed the people of the city, assembled either in the church or in some public place, in
a speech remarkable for the evils it exposes, the boldness with which they are denounced, and the singular
frankness with which the speaker lays bare his most
secret griefs and temptations, showing how truly he
had declared to his brother that, if he once accepted
the bishopric, he should have no more privacy in his
life.[1]

He began by applying his newly-acquired art of
Scripture quotation to the old problem which he had
long before endeavoured to solve,—the compatibility
of Divine providence with human responsibility.
He shows how in the Old Testament terrible races
became instruments in the hands of God for the
punishment of the Jews; yet the king of Babylon
himself was an object of the Divine displeasure.[2]
If the fact that they had served some Divine purpose
might be alleged in excuse of evil-doers, even the
crime of Judas might be justified. But this is not

---

[1] Κατὰ 'Ανδρονίκου. Printed among his letters as Ep. 57,
but evidently a public speech.

[2] His manner of quotation is characteristic : "I do not
remember the exact words, but I feel sure that somewhere in
the Bible, God is represented to have spoken so and so."

the teaching of the Scriptures. It belongs to the
Divine Providence to bring good out of evil, and to
use evil men for good purposes. But these men do
not act as willing servants of God, and their disposi-
tions are hateful to Him. There are "vessels to
honour and to dishonour"; and no man is bound to
make himself a scourge in the hands of Providence.
All work of a destructive character, however overruled,
must be hateful to the Creator. But those who
suffer under the scourge are not thus hateful, for they
are thought worthy of visitation and correction.
The Pentapolis had suffered lately under many
scourges. There had been a plague of locusts, until
a strong wind had arisen and carried them away to
the sea. And there had been the invasion of the
Ausurians, whom God had chastised by the hand of
a noble and skilful general. But a yet more destructive plague was the terrible governor Andronicus,
from whom as yet no deliverance had been obtained.
To himself personally the governor had been the
cause of unwonted troubles and temptations, to
explain which Synesius brought before the people
the story of his past life and his present sorrows.
He told them how, from his early youth, he had
loved leisure and peaceful meditation ; and how, on
coming to man's estate, he had still lived in retirement, though able to accomplish much both for
cities and for individuals by his power of persuasion.
He described the reluctance with which he had
consented to a change and accepted the bishopric,
thereby losing all peace of mind. He had feared
lest he should prove an unworthy minister of the

altar, and his worst fears had been realised. A host
of troubles had come upon him, and the leader of
them all was Andronicus. While this wretch was
making the whole city a place of torment, and
shedding more blood than had been spilt by the old
Spartans at the altar of Artemis, the bishop had been
warning and denouncing him in vain, and been
brought to realise his own weakness. "Anguish in
my soul, a multitude of cares, the vain semblance of
business, and God afar off. If it was by the machinations of evil spirits that these things were done by
Andronicus, they have accomplished whatsoever they
would. Nor could I, as formerly, find comfort in
prayer. For while I seemed to pray, I was carried
away by all manner of cares, divided among rage
and grief and all conflicting feelings. Yet it is by
the mind (Νοῦς) alone that we can approach God,—
the tongue serves only to communicate between man
and man. And, while I could not compose my mind
to prayer, my trial was at hand. . . . . I beheld him
dead whom I had hoped to precede in death."[1]
With singular openness, he went on to tell them how

---

[1] It is not quite clear from this and other passages whether
Synesius meant that if he could have prayed, his child would
not have been taken from him, or that his inability to pray
rendered him incapable of bearing up under the trial. The
latter view seems most consistent with his character, though
the former might find its parallel in his letters. It may be
observed that parts of this speech are word for word the same
with part of a letter to his friend Anastasius,—just as his letter to
Olympius about the bishopric corresponds to his address to the
clergy. In both cases the private letter seems to have been
written first.

he had been tempted to suicide, and restrained, not
by reflection, but by the necessity of action.

After dilating a little on the crimes of Andronicus,
and on the insults he was offering to the Church and
to the bishop—(he affects to disregard personal
indignities, but his pride in his descent from Hercules
can hardly be suppressed)—he brings forward a practical suggestion by which at least his own position
may be made more tolerable.   He wishes to give up
all duties that are not of a purely clerical nature.
His own desire is to be able to keep himself aloof
from the evils which he cannot prevent.   Episcopal
dignity and political activity cannot fitly be combined.
True, in the old times, among both Egyptians and
Jews, the priesthood and the civil government were
united.   But now matters are changed.   Few men
can keep their minds calm and their attention fixed
on sacred things if they are obliged to be constantly
conversant with worldly business.   By contemplation
only is the soul freed from the pollution of matter
and made fit to receive the Divine indwelling
Presence.   It must obey the injunction "Be at
leisure, and know that I am God."[1]   It may be
possible for the strongest and purest natures to live
undefiled amid corruption, but such purity were
above that of the angels.   For if an angel could have
lived for more than thirty years among men without
acquiring any material stain, there would have been
no need for the coming down of the Son of God.
Passing from this curious reflection, which might
easily have brought upon him a charge of heterodoxy,

[1] Septuagint rendering of Psalm xlvi. 10.

L 2

Synesius asserted that, at least in his own case, the active and contemplative functions had proved incompatible. He could not serve two masters, and in attempting to do two kinds of work he was doing both badly. He had never been a popular philosopher nor a public speaker, and he did not wish to be a popular priest. He had not been a good manager of his own estate, and he did not wish to have to manage those of others. But he was willing to devote himself wholly to his sacerdotal functions, reserving to himself the right of choosing the moment when he might come forward with the hope of accomplishing some good end. If he were able to live a life of devotion and contemplation, he might be of great service in giving advice to men aspiring after a higher life. He might even, by occasional intervention in public affairs, make himself useful to the people. But, in general, active business can be well done only by the man whose heart is in it. There were many who would prefer practical business to a life of contemplation. He desired that one such might be chosen, either to supersede him or to act with him as coadjutor. Not that he intended to resign his bishopric,—Andronicus should not prevail thus far. But even if the suggestion as to the appointment of a colleague for practical affairs were not immediately accepted, it might be reserved for future consideration. If it were a novel proposition,[1] that

---

[1] The appointment of a coadjutor would not have been a novelty (see instance in Clausen, "De Syn.," sect. 27), but Synesius was not much versed in the annals of the Church.

was not a decisive argument, as there cannot be a
precedent found for every expedient adopted in time
of need. He concluded by reading the sentence
which the assembly of the clergy had passed against
Andronicus and his adherents.

This remarkable document [1] is one of the earliest
specimens of a sentence of excommunication, and is
in the form of a letter addressed by the bishop and
the church of Ptolemais to all churches everywhere.
Though emanating from a synod, it is expressed in
a form which plainly reveals the leading hand of the
metropolitan. It begins with a vigorous denunciation : "Let Andronicus of Berenice, born and bred
to be the curse of the Pentapolis, who has by corrupt
means obtained the rule over his native land, be
held and accounted of no man for a Christian ; but
let him and all his be shut out from the whole
Church, as those that are hateful to God." It re-
capitulates the cruelties of the governor, calling him
a worse oppressor than Phalaris of Agrigentum, or
Cephren of Egypt, or Sennacherib of Babylon.[2] It
mentions his affronts offered to the Church. His
notices on the church doors are worse than Pilate's
superscription on the cross, for that, at least, was
verbally true. It declares that he and Thoas,
with their adherents, having been warned in vain,
must now be cut off as useless members, lest they
corrupt the whole body. "To Andronicus and
those that are his, to Thoas and those that are

[1] Ep. 58.
[2] It is not to be expected that Synesius should distinguish
between Babylon and Assyria.

his, let no place be open that is held sacred to
God ; let them be shut out from every temple and
chapel and consecrated enclosure. The Devil hath
no place in Paradise, whence, if he glide in privily,
he is again driven forth. Wherefore I command
every man, whether of public or of private station,
not to dwell under the same roof with him nor to
eat at the same table. More especially, I command
the priests not to speak to these men when living,
nor to follow them to the grave when dead. And
if any man shall despise our Church, as that of a
small city, and shall receive those whom she hath
denounced, thinking that she who is poor may be
lightly esteemed, let him know that he is dividing
the Church which Christ willeth to be one. And
such a one, be he Levite or presbyter or bishop,
shall be to us as Andronicus himself; nor will we
give him the right hand of fellowship, nor eat with
him at the same table. And far shall it be from us to
share the sacred mysteries with such as desire to have
aught in common with Andronicus and with Thoas."

Either the vigorous expressions of this decree, or
the general disaffection against the governor to which
it gave voice, was not without effect on the cowardly
nature of Andronicus, and he determined to bow
before the storm. By professions of penitence, he
tried to prevent the circulation of a document which
would be so detrimental to his reputation. He actually succeeded—whether or not by fair means we
cannot tell—in persuading the majority of the bishops
and clergy in the assembly, that if they would defer
the circulation of this decree, he would 'mend his

ways.   Synesius was not so easily convinced, yet he
did not desire to maintain his own opinion too rigidly
against men who were generally his superiors in age
and experience.   He commuted the sentence from
what was called the greater excommunication, which
involved entire exclusion from the churches, to the
lesser, which excluded from the Communion, but not
from the *Missa Catechumenorum*.   At the same time,
he warned the offender that a relapse into his previous courses would be immediately followed by the
issue of the encyclical letter already drawn up against
him.   Andronicus was ready to promise all that was
desired.   But his conduct soon justified the fears of
the bishop.   He became even more violent in his
actions than before, ordered a general proscription,
brought many rich men to beggary by his merciless
extortions, and drove into banishment a young man
of good family—(it must be acknowledged that, in the
eyes of Synesius, a crime was by no means rendered
less heinous by the noble birth of the sufferer)—because he would not dispose of his property according
to the governor's orders.   The metropolitan thereupon
wrote a circular letter to the bishops, ordering that the
execution of the sentence should no longer be delayed.[1]

We have, unfortunately, no means of tracing the
effects of this letter, but it seems certain that the
opposition which the bishop had encouraged while
he kept within the limits of moral and spiritual censure brought about the fall of the governor.   When,
some time after the excommunication, Synesius had
again occasion to address an assembly of his fellow-

[1] Ep. 72.

citizens, Andronicus had been succeeded by Gennadius,[1] probably the same just and able ruler who had preceded him in office. A subsequent letter from Synesius to Theophilus shows that the miserable man met his deserts, and also shows how completely free from vindictiveness was the character of the metropolitan, who afterwards comes forward as the advocate of his bitter foe, endeavouring to obtain for him the justice which he had denied to others. He had delivered him from his perilous position, and now commended him to the care of the archbishop, whose authority was probably necessary to remit the ecclesiastical penalty and to prevent the execution of private vengeance under the pretext of zeal for the Church.

But the fall of Andronicus did not restore peace and order to the Pentapolis. The bad military arrangements of the province rendered any improvements in civil affairs almost nugatory. We have already seen that before the election of Synesius and his conflict with Andronicus, the land had been devastated by a wild Libyan race, the Ausurians, who had, however, received a temporary check from the hand of the brave young general Anysius. The deeds of this skilful leader seem almost fabulous. It is hard to believe that with a band of forty Unnigard mercenaries he can have effectually restrained an enemy that was able shortly afterwards to bring five thousand camels to carry away the spoil captured by their bands of horsemen. It is hard to understand, also, why Synesius, usually so averse to

---

[1] *i.e.*, if the superscription to Catastasis i. is correct.

the employment of mercenaries, should have made an
exception in this case; and again how, if these men
were really Huns, they can have obtained a reputation
for gentleness and good conduct. But probably the
Unnigards were but the nucleus of a considerable
army, and they were doubtless kept in good discipline
by Anysius, who was both discreet and liberal in his
dealings with his soldiers, and was on one occasion
able to quell a mutiny by his just and careful
management. Between the bishop and the general
very friendly relations existed, of paternal interest on
the one side, of filial and loyal devotion on the other.
One little incident illustrates these relations and also
the hasty yet easy-going temper of Synesius. A
certain Carnas had stolen a horse,[1] and then offered
a little money in exchange, which he declined to pay
when the owners refused to sell the animal. Synesius
wrote to Anysius for his help in seizing the offender.[2]
Carnas was not to set himself above the laws, as if
he were a tyrant like Agathocles or Dionysius. He
must be sent to Synesius, and his accusers summoned
against him. Anysius complied with the bishop's
request. But when Carnas was brought before him,
and besought forgiveness, Synesius let him go free,
considering that it was not suitable for a bishop to
prosecute a man during the season of Lent. At the
same time he was anxious for Anysius to understand
that no blame attached to the man into whose custody
Carnas had been committed. Considering his friendship for the general and his constant anxiety on

[1] Ep. 14.   [2] Ep. 6.

behalf of his country, we may, perhaps, regard as
the one proud and happy day of the episcopate of
Synesius that on which he attended and spoke at a
gathering of the people of the Pentapolis to celebrate
their joyful deliverance. He addressed the assembly[1]
in terms of warm congratulation, celebrated in glowing
language the noble deeds of Anysius, declaring that
if he were continued in office and allowed a force of
two hundred Unnigards, he might speedily take the
offensive, and penetrate into the country of the
barbarians. Most unfortunately, however, the suggestion of Synesius was not accepted by those in
power. Anysius was recalled[2] and the claims of the
mercenaries neglected.[3] A leader named Innocentius,[4]
too old and inactive to accomplish much, or to restore
the military arrangements which had been ruined by
the previous bad management of Cerealius, was sent
out in the place of the young hero. Under these
circumstances, the barbarians repeated and redoubled
their ravages. Not only did they now carry away all
the plunder they could lay their hands on, but they
also seized the young children, and took them to
train with their own, so that in future days they
might wage a parricidal warfare against their own
country. The soldiers were few and scattered, the
leadership utterly inefficient. Another meeting of
the people was held, and the bishop again assisted
them in drawing up a complaint to be sent to
Anthemius at Constantinople. Strong representations

---

[1] Catastasis ii., which seems chronologically prior to Catastasis i.

[2] Ep. 59, &c.　　　　[3] Ep. 78.　　　　[4] Catastasis i.

were made of the desperate state of the country, and
of the probability that it would soon be lost to the
empire completely, and an urgent request was sent
for at least four centuries of men with a competent
general. The address is not framed in Synesius's
happiest style. We might well have spared his descriptions of his personal experiences, — his night
alarms, his fevered dreams, his thoughts of flight
even to a place where no man knew his lineage—(it
is to be feared that wherever Synesius had taken
refuge, the inhabitants would not long have remained
in ignorance of his descent from Hercules)—his final
resolution to die at his post. But his lamentations
and expressions of fear were those of a rhetorician,
not of a coward. He wrote to his brother that he
was busy in the work of defence, frequently visiting
the fortifications, acting towards the guards rather as
a fellow-soldier than as a priest. It was probably at
this time that Bishop Isidore of Pelusium wrote to
encourage him, and to remove his scruples as to
uniting military and ecclesiastical duties by citing the
examples of Old Testament worthies.[1] He certainly
needed all the encouragement that could be given to
him. A second domestic calamity had befallen
him,—the death of another of his children. But yet
again his efforts for the common good distracted his
thoughts from his private sorrows. We do not know

---

[1] In the works of Isidore there are four letters addressed to
Synesius, though we have none of Synesius addressed to him.
It is interesting to find that Synesius was on friendly terms with
an orthodox ecclesiastic of high repute and an opponent of
Theophilus.

when or how the barbarians retreated. But as
Synesius was certainly not—according to his own
forebodings—the last bishop of Ptolemais, it is
probable that the Ausurians, unwilling to encounter
a prolonged resistance, desisted from their attempts
to conquer the capital of the province, and, as before,
departed with their booty, leaving a precarious respite
to the citizens.[1]

Yet, after all, he felt that the country was doomed,
and that none of his efforts could avert its fate. It
seemed as if he had lost all domestic happiness and
all peace of mind, and received in exchange a life of
fruitless efforts and an overwhelming sense of failure.
Yet the student of his life need not share his own
belief, that his earlier were better than his latter
days. Crushed with a sense of personal impotence
before the merciless oppression of the governor and
the devastating ravages of the enemy, overwhelmed
with domestic troubles, incapable of hope or of
prayer,—he is yet, in his unwearied efforts for the
relief of his distressed fellow-citizens, a nobler spec-
tacle in our eyes than when, in the full enjoyment of
family prosperity and studious leisure, he was spinning
out fine-drawn arguments to prove an unimportant
thesis, or indulging his carefully-fostered religious
sentiment in fanciful metaphysical hymns.

---

[1] Perhaps the worthy Marcellinus, mentioned in Ep. 62,
effected this retreat. It is not easy to see whether he held the
office of *dux* or of *præses*.

CHAPTER VIII.

LAST DAYS OF SYNESIUS—CONCLUSION.

Ὁ τοιοῦτος [σοφὸς] οὖν οὐκ ἂν ἀπογνοίη τῶν αὐτῶν κινημάτων ἐπανιόντων συνεπίεται τὰ αἰτιατὰ τοῖς αἰτίοις, καὶ βίους ἐν γῇ, τοὺς αὐτοὺς εἶναι τοῖς πάλαι, καὶ γενέσεις, καὶ τροφὰς, καὶ γνώμας, καὶ τύχας.

THE events which occurred during the episcopal rule of Synesius seem sufficiently important and various to fill a much larger period than they actually occupied. There is only one of his letters which seems to have been written after the death of Theophilus,—an exhortation to a certain Cyril, who had been suffering under a temporary excommunication (not, of course, the celebrated Cyril, nephew and successor of Theophilus), to return to the Church, into which he would certainly have been readmitted if the venerable man who had excluded him had lived a little longer. As Theophilus died in 412 A.D., and Synesius was, as we have seen, most probably elected to the episcopate about the end of 409 A.D., all the events of his episcopal life of which we have any record, with the possible exception of the great invasion of the Ausurians, fall within the space of three years. They were for him years, it has been

---

[1] Synesius, "De Providentia," II., c. 7.

clearly shown, of bitter conflict without and within,
and the last of the trials which we know to have
befallen him was not the least hard to bear. His
only surviving son, who he had fondly hoped would
be the prop of his old age, soon followed the other
two. The last letters of Synesius express his bitter
sense of bereavement. To his male friends he
professed a resignation rather Stoic than Christian,
and seemed still to feel some interest in other affairs;
but to the womanly heart of Hypatia he entrusted
the full measure of his woe.[1] He felt utterly broken
down in body as in mind. His strength was ebbing
away, and his only desire for himself was, " Would
that I might either die, or cease to think upon the
grave of my children !" Whether or no Synesius
was really at the point of death when he wrote this
letter we cannot tell. He seems frequently to have
suffered from physical infirmities, yet hitherto he had
always recovered, and he was still a comparatively
young man. The absence, however, of any letters
from him to Cyril incline us to think that he did not
long survive the Archbishop Theophilus. It is almost
certain that he did not live till the year 431 A.D., as
in that year a council was held at Ephesus to put
down the heresy of Nestorius, and the bishop of Ptolemais present on that occasion bore the name, not of
Synesius, but of Euoptius. We naturally conclude
that this man was the brother and correspondent of
his predecessor, though it is certainly difficult to conceive how, after the murder of Hypatia, one of her

---

[1] Ep. 70, 126, 6.

pupils can have consented to hold office under Cyril.
A conjecture may be allowed to us, in the absence of
material for historic proof, that the people of Ptolemais may have acquiesced in the request of Synesius
for a coadjutor, and have sought to relieve his
troubles by appointing his beloved brother to lighten
his labours. In this case, on the death of the metropolitan, his coadjutor might naturally have succeeded
to the whole of the previously-divided functions.
A further suggestion may be made, not that it rests
on any proof, but that it is not impossibly true, and
certainly pleasing to dwell upon. In one of the last
letters of Synesius, written after the loss of his only
remaining son, he appears busy in collecting the
necessary furniture for some hermitage or place of
retreat.[1] If this was for himself, it seems not wholly
improbable that he may have been able to attain his
cherished desire,—to leave most of the active work
of his see in more practical hands, and to retire to a
life of solitary prayer and meditation, in which his
unhinged mind might recover its balance, might
resume the speculations of the past in the light added
by recent experiences, and might labour to achieve a
more harmonious union between the doctrines of the
schools and those of the Church. We do not know
whether he ever heard the fate of his beloved
instructress, which would probably have gone further
towards breaking his heart than all the evils which
had hitherto befallen him. It happened two years
after the accession of Cyril, and it seems most

---

[1] 'Ασκητήριον.

probable that before that time the weary man had obtained one of the two things he most desired,— either the peace of a retired life or else the peace of death.

It is to be expected that a man of so many-sided a character and so varied a life should be regarded in many different aspects by contemporaries and by successive generations of posterity. It seems almost impossible that so amiable a man should have bitter enemies; yet there are not wanting some who have represented him as a heathen wolf who intruded into the Christian fold. If we accept their opinion, we must allow that it is the first case known to history in which a wolf was, by the shepherd, driven into the fold against his will, and, once within, devoted all his energies to prevent the sheep from being too closely shorn. The more friendly, but perhaps scarcely more appreciative, view of Gibbon has already been stated. The sceptical historian could esteem the courage and admire the talents of the philosopher-bishop, but could not enter into his aspirations, nor do justice to his religious sincerity. And, like many men of mark, Synesius has suffered much at the hands of his friends, especially at those of orthodox Catholics. It is very strange to find that, not very long after his death, a completely mythical personage had assumed his name and place in Church legend, bearing even less resemblance to the original than does the legendary Dietrich of Berne to the historical Theodoric. By a remarkable irony of fate, he is represented as converting a heathen philosopher to beliefs which the actual Synesius did not himself

hold, and especially as insisting on the literal character of the promise : "He that giveth to the poor
lendeth to the Lord,"—going so far as to draw up,
in the name of Christ, a promissory note to the rich
almsgiver, which he, in return, was so obliging as to
receipt duly after death, so that the signed document.
found in his coffin was removed to the church,—an
edifying monument to all the faithful ! [1]

The Jesuits, who have devoted much praiseworthy
labour to the elucidation of the works of Synesius,
have not been quite guiltless in this respect, but have
distorted some evident facts so as to minimise the
unorthodoxy of the bishop, and especially his objections to a celibate life. Protestant writers have
generally used him more fairly. The eminently
charitable and tolerant Neander, in his "Denkwürdig-
keiten aus der Geschichte des Christenthums," has
some very pleasing and appreciative remarks on the
transition of Synesius from Platonism to Christianity,
but he seems to go rather further than ascertained
facts will warrant when he assumes the beneficial
and christianising effects on the character of Synesius
of the painful experiences of his later life, and regards
as denoting a real change in his religious views the
difference of language and of simile used in speaking
to men of the ecclesiastical profession by one who
had previously only uttered his thoughts to those

---

[1] The story is told in the Migne edition of Synesius, and in
several other books, including Lecky's "History of European
Morals." If further proof were needed that the story is spurious,
we might point to the fact that the interesting receipt was said
to be kept in the church at *Cyrene.*

who felt as he did. But it is possible, without
attaching any blame to Synesius, or seeking to represent him as more of a philosopher or more of a
Christian than he actually was, to consider him as
an honest, though sometimes erring man, an aspiring
but confused thinker, who, through the force of circumstances, was led in later life to adopt habits and
phrases to which, in his youth, he had been a
stranger,—who yet never relinquished his grasp of
those principles which had first made life to have
a meaning for him, and always regarded with com-
parative indifference the form in which doctrines
might be clothed, provided that they really agreed
with the truths recognised by philosophy in every
guise. Several influences may have tended to make
the use of those new habits and phrases come more
naturally to him as time went on :—the constant use
of the Liturgy, the society of men brought up in
Christian principles, the experience of conflicts with
depravity and wickedness, which might bring home
to him the need for renovation in the world at large
and in the individual soul. For, though it might be
an exaggeration to say that Andronicus made him a
better Christian by forcing him to believe in the
Devil, it is certainly true that one of the chief differences which distinguished the Christians from the
last generation of pagans was their deeper sense of
human corruption and need of deliverance ; and this
sense could be in no way more effectually aroused
than by a long struggle against enormities like those
of the terrible enemies and yet more terrible rulers
of the Pentapolis. If we were asked which passage

in the works of Synesius show the nearest approxi-
mation to a Christian tone of thought and feeling,
we should point to the short hymn[1] addressed to
Christ as Healer and Light-giver, and to the really
fine outburst in one of the letters to Theophilus
against degrading Christian solemnities to the level
of magic incantations.[2] But a parallel may be found
to the former in some of his most thoroughly Neo-
Platonic verses, and to the latter in his expressions
in the treatise "Concerning Dreams" as to the
superiority of a pure life over proficiency in occult
arts. Again, when he would show to the people the
dignity of human life by reminding them that Christ
died for all, rather than by referring to the existence
of a divine spark in every human mind, the reason
is probably not, as Neander would have it, that he
was acquiring Christian modes of thought, but rather
that he felt obliged to express his meaning in terms
that ordinary Christian people would best understand.

It may seem to some critics that the religion or
philosophy of Synesius was but a feeble prop and
guide, seeing that it failed him at the moment of
his greatest need, when he sunk into a despondent
belief that fate was against him and that God had
abandoned him. But we, who are by no means
bound to share that belief, may explain the apparent
spiritual failure of Synesius by the facts we know as
to his temperament and early training. The philosophy on which he had been nourished placed the

---

[1] Hymn X.   [2] Ep. 67.

summum bonum in contemplation, and not in action. His own natural disposition was decidedly favourable to this view. Not that he was by nature of a calm and contemplative mind, but rather that the facility with which his thoughts were distracted and the irritability of his feelings rendered it impossible for him to live in continual consciousness of the truths which he most earnestly believed, unless he was able frequently to revive his spiritual faculties in seasons of calm retirement. When public cares deprived him of his beloved leisure, he felt constantly in a state of distraction. He never fell into the abysses of scepticism ; still less did he take up an attitude of rebellious defiance. He might wish to die, but not to curse God first. He seems not to have doubted that his former peace and confidence might be recovered, if only he could have opportunities of seeking it in his accustomed ways. We may acknow- ledge that this is not the very highest type of religious life, but it was free from any admixture of hypocrisy or insincerity. Synesius himself was ready to allow that a riper spiritual nature than his might be subject to fewer imperative spiritual needs. His religion was not of the kind that could convert the barbarians, renovate a corrupt society, and raise uncultured men to the moral level of heroes and saints : it was the religion of a cultivated eclectic, and should be esti- mated, as to its points of strength and of weakness, in relation to the man himself and the circumstances under which he lived.

If he was not a saint, neither was he a hero nor yet a powerful thinker, although there were elements in his character such as are seldom found in any but in spiritual and practical heroes. His character attracts us by its many amiable and delightful qualities, while it occasionally disappoints us by its utter want of balance. But, at least, he had followed the Delphic precept, and understood his own nature and the root of his shortcomings. His great defect was a want of calm. His mind was eager to receive all manner of truths, but could not dwell on them long enough to fuse them into a consistent system. His moral nature was easily aroused at the sight of injustice or cowardice, but he was generally too ready to let offenders go free. His whole soul was set on the right performance of the tasks which he accepted as divinely appointed and on the attainment of spiritual perfection. Yet his heart too soon sank within him when the means he was pursuing seemed not to be leading to the desired goal, and was far too dependent for energy and hopefulness on the appearance of success without and on the enjoyment of comfort within. He himself said to Hypatia that he was only fit to live so long as he was inexperienced in the woes of life.[1] There was something womanish, he said to another friend, in his sensitiveness to domestic trouble.[2] In practical life he seems a dreamer, while in speculation he seems somewhat of a dilettante. Yet, if these faults do not strongly repel us, it is because they are accompanied by a warm and loving temperament, a mind saturated with Greek literature, a lofty idealism in theory, and a strong desire to

---

[1] Ep. 16. [2] Ep. 79.

attain it in practice. The fascination of his whole
character can only be understood by a sympathetic
student of his life and works.

The life and the writings of Synesius are worthy of
study on several accounts. They throw unexpected
light on many points connected with the civil and the
ecclesiastical order—or disorder—of the times, on
interesting phases of social life and transitional forms
of thought. But the reader who begins the study for
the purpose of historical investigation is liable to be
attracted into the region of psychological inquiry,
that he may seek for some light on the development
of so peculiar a mind and character ; and, before long,
he may find that all scientific interest in the subject
is less strong than the charm exercised on the imagination by the story of so strangely pathetic a life. Men
of the type of Synesius, who have left a record of all
their varied experiences,—their hopeful and their
desperate efforts, their merits and their faults, their
joys and sorrows and aspirations,—do more than any
others to help us to realise the continuity of human
life. They bridge for us the gulf which separates the
present from the past, not merely by giving us vivid
descriptions of the world in which they lived, and by
setting forth before us the ideas which in their days
prevailed in the world of mind, but also by appealing
directly to our human sympathies and kindling
within us feelings of personal affection and respect.

APPENDIX I.

—◆◇◆—

HYMN II.

YET again the light of morning,
Yet again the day appeareth ;
Gone the wandering shades of darkness,
Yet again arise, my spirit ;
Rise to God, and sing His praises,
Who delights the morn with daylight,
Who the night with stars rejoiceth,
Stars around the world revolving.

Darkness lay, obscure and pregnant,
Hidden in the lap of Æther,
While on purest fire she rested,
Where the Moon revolves in glory,
Driving round the inmost circle.
And above the eight-fold circling
Of the spheres of stars and planets
Rolls the stream serene and starless,
Bearing in its mighty bosom
All their strange, conflicting courses,
Round the Mind that governs all things,
Shrouding in its spotless pinions

Those far limits of creation.
And beyond, the blessed Silence
Parts the realms of Mind and Wisdom,
Parts, yet ever keeps united.

One the Root and One the Fountain,
Rising in a threefold splendour.
Where in depths untold the Father,
There the glorious Son is with Him,
Offspring of His heart mysterious,
And the Wisdom all-creative,
And the Light that binds in oneness
Of the Holy Spirit shineth.
One the Root and One the Fountain
Whence the stream of good outpoureth,
Whence a race above all substance,
Issuing eager towards creation,
Others too, in space abiding,
Blessed, light-dispensing spirits.
Thence, within the bounds of Nature,
All the choir of deathless rulers
Hymned the glory of the Father,
Sang the Image first-begotten,
In a strain of heavenly wisdom.
Near to them, their kindly parents,
Comes the host of deathless angels,
Some, in rapture beatific,
Gazing on the Form of Beauty,
Others watching spheres and orbits,
Ruling all the course of Nature,
Bearing down to worlds of matter

Something of the highest order,
E'en where Nature, downward sinking,
Brings to life the hosts of dæmons,
Many-voiced, in wiles abounding.
Thence the Heroes, thence proceedeth
Air that all the world encircles,
Giving life to all things breathing,
Strangely divers forms of creatures.

All the world is by Thy counsel
Still sustained, thou Root of all things,
All that is and all that has been,
All that shall be, all that can be.
Thou art Father, Thou art Mother,
Thou art Male and Thou art Female,
Thou art Voice and Thou art Silence,
Thou art Nature's inmost Nature,
Thou art Lord, the Age of Ages.
If I dare to call upon Thee,
I would hail Thee, Root of Order,
Hail of all things thou the Centre,
Unity of heavenly numbers,
Of the lords before creation.
Glory to Thee, as 'tis fitting
That a God should ever glory.
Turn Thine ear to me in pity,
Listen to my rhythmic measures,
Beam on me the light of Wisdom,
Shed the riches of Thy glory,
Shed on me the grace abundant
Of a life at peace from tumult.
Need and hardship come not nigh me,

Nor the cares of worldly riches.
O defend my frame from sickness
And the rush of restless passions.
Keep away the woe and anguish
That devours the mind and spirit.
So no earthly care may hinder
My blest soul ascending upward;
Rising then on airy pinion,
I shall share the secret honours
Of the Son's most holy service.

HYMN X.

CHRIST think upon me,
Son of the Highest
Heavenly Ruler,
Think on Thy servant,
Sinful and wretched,
Calling upon Thee.
Grant me release from the
Tumult of passions,
Death-bringing evils,
Rooted within my
Spirit polluted.
Saviour Jesus,
Let me behold Thy
Radiant glory.
Then will I clearly
Sound forth Thy praises,
Thou the soul's healer,
Healer of bodies.
Praise to the Father
And to the Spirit.

APPENDIX II.

---◆◇◆---

CHRONOLOGICAL SUMMARY OF CHIEF EVENTS DURING
THE LIFE OF SYNESIUS.

Dates A.D.	General History.	Church History.	Personal History of Synesius.
375	Death of Valentinian I., Emperor of the West. His young son, Valentinian II., is associated with Gratian in the Western Empire, while their uncle, Valens, continues to rule in the East.	Goths converted to Christianity through the labours of the Arian Bishop Ulfilas.	Circ. Birth of Synesius of Cyrene.
376 } 377 }	Inroads of Goths, driven south by the Huns. War on the Danube.	Valens ceases to persecute the Homoousians.	(It must be remembered that the dates in this column are not in all cases clearly ascertained. The chronology followed is generally that of Clausen.)
378	Gratian defeats the Allemanni, but Valens is defeated by the Goths at Hadrianople, and killed in the battle.		
379	Theodosius is by Gratian made Emperor of the East. The Imperial forces gain advantages over the Goths.		
380		Theodosius baptised by the Homoousian bishop of Thessalonica.	
381		Second Œcumenical Council held at Constantinople. Nicene Creed reasserted.	
382	Final submission of the West Goths. Many join the imperial host.	Decrees against Arians.	

DATES A.D.	GENERAL HISTORY.	CHURCH HISTORY.	PERSONAL HISTORY OF SYNESIUS.
383	Insurrection of Maximus in Britain. Flight and assassination of Gratian.	Synod of various sects at Constantinople. Victory of the Homoousians.	
384 385		Ambrose of Milan opposes the Emperor Justina.	
386 387 388	Maximus invades Italy, but is defeated, captured, and put to death by Theodosius.	Arian tumults in Constantinople. Sedition at Antioch. Flavian, the bishop, intercedes with the emperor for the city.	
389		Paganism harshly put down in Alexandria by the Archbishop Theophilus.	
390 391	Sedition and massacre of Thessalonica.	Ambrose obliges Theodosius to do penance. All heathen sacrifices prohibited.	
392 393 394	Valentinian II. murdered at Vienna, in Gaul. Eugenius usurps the empire of the West, but is defeated and put to death by Theodosius.		About this time Synesius comes to Alexandria, and becomes the pupil of Hypatia.
395 396	Death of Theodosius. His sons succeed him: Arcadius in the East, Honorius in the West. Fall and death of Rufinus. Eutropius becomes chief minister of Arcadius. Alaric the Goth invades and plunders Greece.		
397	Temporary check of Alaric by Stilicho.		Synesius, having returned to Cyrene, is sent on an embassy to Constantinople.
398	Alaric made king of the Visigoths.	John Chrysostom made bishop of Constantinople.	
399	Rebellion of Tribigild the Goth, followed by that of Gainas.		Synesius, waiting for an audience, writes the first part of "De Providentia."

Dates A.D.	General History.	Church History.	Personal History of Synesius.
400	Fall of Eutropius. Banishment of Aurelian and Saturninus. The Goths in Constantinople. Their panic and flight. Death of Gainas. Alaric invades Italy.	Chrysostom tries to reform the clergy.	He delivers, before Arcadius, the oration, "De Regno." He composes, for Paeonius, "De Dono Astrolabii." Leaves Constantinople during an earthquake, and returns, after a dangerous voyage, to Cyrene. Makes a pilgrimage into the Libyan Desert, and writes Hymn III.
401		Theophilus quarrels with the *Long Monks.* Condemnation of the works of Origen.	The Pentapolis overrun by barbarians. Synesius writes, "De Providentia," Part II.
402			Synesius visits Athens.
403	Stilicho again defeats Alaric.	Chrysostom persecuted by the Empress Eudocia, and sent into exile by the synod of Chalcedon. He returns after a popular tumult, and is again banished.	Synesius goes to Alexandria to be married. Writes "Dion," "De Insomniis," and "Cynegeticæ."
404			Synesius takes refuge from the Macetæ in a fortified place. Bad conduct of the captain, Cerealius.
405			Synesius takes an active part in the preparations for war, which are rendered useless by the cowardice of the captain, John.
406	Italy and Gaul invaded by German hosts. Defeat of the chief, Radagais, by Stilicho.		Synesius retreats to a country estate near the salt-pits of Ammon.
407		Death of Chrysostom.	[During this period of his life, he writes "Calvitii Encomium," most of his Hymns, and almost all his private letters which are extant.]

Dates A.D.	General History.	Church History.	Personal History of Synesius.
408	Alaric before Rome. Stilicho murdered in a palace intrigue. Death of Arcadius. His young son, Theodosius II., succeeds. Firm administration of Anthemius.		
409	Second siege of Rome by the Goths.		Synesius elected bishop of Ptolemais. Eight months allowed him for decision.
410	Third siege of Rome by the Goths. Death of Alaric.		Synesius goes to Alexandria to be ordained and consecrated. Makes a visitation of his diocese.
	Roman troops withdrawn from Britain.		Holds an assembly to congratulate Anysius on his victories over the Ausurians. Excommunicates the governor, Andronicus. Death of one of his children.
411			Death of another of the sons of Synesius. The country again ravaged by the Ausurians. Synesius calls an assembly, and draws up a complaint to be sent to Anthemius.
412	Adolf, successor to Alaric, leads the Goths into Spain.	Death of Theophilus of Alexandria. Cyril succeeds.	[The fragments of Homilies of Synesius and Hymn X. probably date from about this time.]
413		Breach between Cyril and the praefect Orestes (which afterwards led to the murder of Hypatia by the Alexandrian monks and populace.)	Death of the last remaining child of Synesius. Sickness of Synesius, which probably ended in his death.

WYMAN AND SONS, PRINTERS,
GREAT QUEEN STREET, LINCOLN'S INN FIELDS,
LONDON, W.C.

PUBLICATIONS

OF THE

Society for Promoting Christian Knowledge.

THE

FATHERS FOR ENGLISH READERS.

A Series of Monographs on the Chief Fathers of the Church, the
Fathers selected being centres of influence at important
periods of Church History and in important
spheres of action.

Fcap. 8vo., cloth boards, 2s. each.

LEO THE GREAT.
By the Rev. CHARLES GORE, M.A.

GREGORY THE GREAT.
By the Rev. J. BARMBY, B.D.

SAINT AMBROSE : his Life, Times, and Teaching.
By the Rev. ROBINSON THORNTON, D.D.

SAINT AUGUSTINE.
By the Rev. E. L. CUTTS, B.A.

SAINT BASIL THE GREAT.
By the Rev. RICHARD T. SMITH, B.D.

SAINT HILARY OF POITIERS, AND SAINT MARTIN OF TOURS.
By the Rev. J. GIBSON CAZENOVE, D.D.

SAINT JEROME.
By the Rev. EDWARD L. CUTTS, B.A

SAINT JOHN OF DAMASCUS.
By the Rev. J. H. LUPTON, M.A.

THE APOSTOLIC FATHERS.
By the Rev. H. S. HOLLAND.

THE DEFENDERS OF THE FAITH; or, The Christian Apologists of the Second and Third Centuries.
By the Rev. F. WATSON, M.A.

THE VENERABLE BEDE.
By the Rev. G. F. BROWNE.

NON-CHRISTIAN RELIGIOUS SYSTEMS.

A Series of Manuals which furnish in a brief and popular form an accurate account of the great Non-Christian Religious Systems of the World.

Fcap. 8vo., cloth boards, 2s. 6d. each.

Buddhism—Being a Sketch of the Life and Teachings of Guatama, the Buddha.
By T. W. RHYS DAVIDS. With Map.

Buddhism in China.
By the Rev. S. BEAL. With Map.

Confucianism and Taouism.
By Professor ROBERT K. DOUGLAS, of the British Museum. With Map.

Hinduism.
By Professor MONIER WILLIAMS. With Map.

Islam and its Founder.
By J. W. H. STOBART. With Map.

The Corán—Its Composition and Teaching, and the Testimony it bears to the Holy Scriptures.
By Sir WILLIAM MUIR, K.C.S.I.

THE HEATHEN WORLD AND ST. PAUL.

This Series is intended to throw light upon the Writings and Labours of the Apostle of the Gentiles.

Fcap. 8vo., cloth boards, 2s. each.

St. Paul in Greece.
By the Rev. G. S. DAVIES. With Map.

St. Paul in Damascus and Arabia.
By the Rev. GEORGE RAWLINSON, M.A., Canon of Canterbury. With Map.

St. Paul at Rome.
By the Very Rev. CHARLES MERIVALE, D.D., D.C.L., Dean of Ely. With Map.

St. Paul in Asia Minor and at the Syrian Antioch.
By the Rev. E. H. PLUMPTRE, D.D. With Map.

THE HOME LIBRARY.

*A Series of Book*s *illustrative of Church History, &c., specially, but not exclusively, adapted for Sunday Reading.*

Crown 8vo., cloth boards, 3s. 6d. each.

Black and White. Mission Stories.
By H. FORDE.

Charlemagne.
By the Rev. E. L. CUTTS, B.A. With Map.

Constantine the Great: The Union of Church and State.
By the Rev. EDWARD L. CUTTS.

Great English Churchmen ; or, Famous Names in English Church History and Literature.
By W. H. DAVENPORT ADAMS.

John Hus. The Commencement of Resistance to Papal Authority on the part of the Inferior Clergy.
By the Rev. A. H. WRATISLAW.

Judæa and her Rulers, from Nebuchadnezzar to Vespasian.
By M. BRAMSTON. With Map.

Military Religious Orders of the Middle Ages ; the Hospitallers, the Templars, the Teutonic Knights, and others.
By the Rev. F. C. WOODHOUSE.

Mitslav ; or, the Conversion of Pomerania.
By the late Right Rev. R. MILMAN, D.D.

Narcissus: A Tale of Early Christian Times.
By the Right Rev. W. BOYD CARPENTER.

Richelieu.
By GUSTAVE MASSON, Esq.

Sketches of the Women of Christendom.
By the Author of " The Chronicles of the Schönberg-Cotta Family."

The Churchman's Life of Wesley.
By R. DENNY URLIN, Esq.

The Church in Roman Gaul.
By the Rev. R. T. SMITH. With Map.

The House of God the Home of Man.
By the Rev. Canon JELF.

The Inner Life, as Revealed in the Correspondence of Celebrated Christians.
Edited by the Rev. T. ERSKINE.

The Life of the Soul in the World : Its Nature, Needs, Dangers, Sorrows, Aids, and Joys.
By the Rev. F. C. WOODHOUSE.

The North African Church.
By the Rev. J. LLOYD. With Map.

Thoughts and Characters ; being Selections from the Writings of the Author of " The Chronicles of the Schönberg-Cotta Family."

CONVERSION OF THE WEST.

A Series of Volumes showing how the Conversion of the Chief Races of the West was brought about, and their condition before this occurred.

Fcap. 8vo., cloth boards, 2s. each.

The Celts.
By the Rev. G. F. MACLEAR, D.D. With Two Maps.

The English.
By the above Author. With Two Maps.

The Northmen.
By the above Author. With Map.

The Slavs.
By the above Author. With Map.

The Continental Teutons.
By the Very Rev. Dean MERIVALE. With Map.

ANCIENT HISTORY FROM THE MONUMENTS.

This Series of Books is chiefly intended to illustrate the Sacred Scriptures by the results of recent Monumental Researches in the East.

Fcap. 8vo., cloth boards, 2s. each.

Assyria, from the Earliest Times to the Fall of Nineveh.
By the late GEORGE SMITH, Esq., of the British Museum.

Sinai: from the Fourth Egyptian Dynasty to the Present Day.
By HENRY S. PALMER, Major R.E., F.R.A.S. With Map.

Babylonia (The History of).
By the late GEORGE SMITH, Esq. Edited by the Rev. A. H. SAYCE.

Greek Cities and Islands of Asia Minor.
By W. S. W. VAUX, M.A.

Egypt, from the Earliest Times to B.C. 300.
By S. BIRCH, LL.D.

Persia, from the Earliest Period to the Arab Conquest.
By W. S. W. VAUX, M.A.

DEPOSITORIES:

NORTHUMBERLAND AVENUE, CHARING CROSS, W.C.;
43, QUEEN VICTORIA STREET, E.C.; 26, ST. GEORGE'S PLACE, S.W.
BRIGHTON: 135, NORTH STREET.

www.ingramcontent.com/pod-product-compliance
Lightning Source LLC
Chambersburg PA
CBHW030553040726

47497CB00008B/2708